ORPHAN IN THE SANDS

by

Virginia Haroutunian

Our past is the key to our present.
Virginia Haroutunian

Cover design by Paul Sagsoorian

Role Manuscript

ISBN 0-9664381-0-8

A lovegift for Hyreeg and Myreeg

ACKNOWLEDGMENTS

Special thanks to Victoria Haroutunian, co-author.

Dr. Kenneth Pitts, mentor, friend and teacher who helped me in exceptional ways to understand my eating disorder.

His Eminence Archbishop Mesrob Ashjian, Dr. Dennis Papazian, Mr. and Mrs. Dickran Toumajian and Ara Sarafian for Armenian historical materials.

And last, Dr. Harry Hahn, Dr. Jane Bingham, Jane Johnson, Nancy Nahabedian and Eric Ninneman for their literary expertise.

Chapter 1

The British White Star liner slowly sailed through the Narrows into Upper New York Bay and stopped at the dock in New York Harbor. Two hours later, Tourvanda Ahigian stood ready to depart from the steamship, clutching only her small suitcase containing family letters, photos, and a box of King George chocolates. It was six o'clock in the morning on a snowy March day in 1928. A cold mist rose from the ocean. She was without coat, boots or gloves.

Twenty men in blue uniforms with thick Brooklyn accents boarded the ship to inspect the first and second class British tourists and immigrants. These British immigrants were not listed as such, as it was obvious from their wealth that they were not likely to become a public charge. They were allowed to enter New York and avoid Ellis Island altogether.

The United States government thought that the steerage class, lower economic groups, were more likely to become public charges. A station was opened in 1892 to carry out the process of immigration and naturalization for the steerage class in New York Harbor. This station became Ellis Island.

While the first and second class passengers were being inspected, the steerage immigrants, including Tourvanda, crowded the deck in hopes of seeing their new country. To her right and left, what looked to be well over five hundred yards, were continuous rows of docks. The harbor was packed with ships of every size from every nation around the world. She loved hearing the deep resonating sound of ships' horns. People were running around the dock; some preparing to spend an afternoon sailing;

others racing about in hopes of obtaining a fishing charter; many more were arriving. Then there were many dressed in suits holding signs with immigrant names on them.

Tourvanda's scanning eyes caught sight of the Statue of Liberty, that majestic symbol of hope for so many immigrants. A half-mile beyond the Statue was Ellis Island, where her fate would be decided. Tourvanda, a homeless refugee from Western Armenia (now Turkish Armenia) had convinced her cousins to bring her to the United States on a visitor's pass. Like all other immigrants, Tourvanda hoped for the opportunity to take up permanent residence. She was concerned by the fact that Cousin Harry was not an official citizen; while it was only a small legal detail, it still meant that they could not sponsor any immigrants because they were not officially legal them-selves.

The confusion stemming from the various peoples and noises were a distraction to Tourvanda, who was intent on finding her relative. She was certain that Cousin Harry would be waiting at the Barge Office, as a ship authority had told her they had sent word to him through telegram announcing her arrival two days in advance. She had only a small photograph of a much younger Harry she'd known as a child.

An authority approached her and politely took her suitcase, informing her that it would be transported to Ellis Island. Tourvanda took in a deep breath, paused for a moment of silent reflection before walking down the gangplank alongside the other immigrants. A tall man with refined masculine features, dressed in a finely tailored brown wool suit, walked over to her and asked with urgency in a distinctly Armenian accent if there were any Armenians on board.

"I'm Armenian," Tourvanda said with interest.

"Do you know Tourvanda Ahigian?"

"I'm Tourvanda Ahigian."

"I'm your cousin Harry." He smiled as he reached out his muscular arms.

They embraced. Tears formed in his enthusiastic dark brown eyes, while for Tourvanda it was a rare moment of impenetrable euphoria. Here standing before her was, to her knowledge, one of two remaining Ahigian relatives left from her days in the Old Country. Tourvanda's joy was brief, however. A uniformed immigration official interrupted the long sought reunion by taking her arm and forcefully leading her away. She looked back at her rediscovered relative with an expression of surprise and confusion. His expression was much the same. She started to cry and Cousin Harry shouted to her, "Don't worry. I'll come back for you." She resisted, but the grasp did not relax until she was in a transport shuttle.

Tourvanda sat down and looked out the window with tears brimming on the edges of her dark brown eyes. The actions of the last few minutes were overwhelming. Anger swelled within her. There had been no opportunity to defend herself and no chance of hearing an explanation from the guards regarding their treatment of her. The thought of returning to Egypt made the moment more ripe for bitterness. She found temporary solace when the barge arrived fifteen minutes later at Ellis Island, meaning that for the time being, at least, she would remain in America.

She managed to notice Ellis Island from the barge. The island seemed hardly higher than the waterline. The building rose out of the water and looked like a palace with its picturesque, turreted towers and red brick. Upon arrival Tourvanda followed the other immigrants into a single-file line, walking under a covered walkway to the front steps of the building leading to the baggage room. She grasped her suitcase and followed the line to the east side of the Great Hall.

There was a maze of aisles formed by iron pipe bars. She followed a group of thirty immigrants to the medical processing area where a nurse examined her scalp, throat, hands, and eyes. She passed the medical test and was led to the registry section where she answered routine questions about her name, birthday, place of birth and the addresses of any relatives who might sponsor her. Three hours later she was taken to the Armenian section of the Hall. No one had yet said if she would be permitted to remain in the United States. She sat stoically next to two girls at a table on the main floor of the Great Hall.

"*Pahrev* (hello)," said one of the girls, who Tourvanda later learned was Arpi. "Where are you from?"

"Pahrev," smiled Tourvanda. It made her feel good to see an Armenian face and to hear her language. "I come from Alexandria, Egypt."

The other girl, Seta, told Tourvanda that they had been on Ellis Island for two months after arriving from Italy. They had a brother who would sponsor them, but still they were made to wait. Their brother, while living in America for eight years, had not obtained his citizenship. Like Cousin Harry, there was no danger of him being sent back, as it was only a matter of paperwork. However, it meant that there was no one who could officially sponsor Arpi and Seta. Tourvanda did not say a word. A public address announcement broke the silence saying dinner was served in the cafeteria.

The cafeteria was at the east end of the Great Hall. It served a variety of American and ethnic foods at no charge—spaghetti, corned beef, cabbage, hot dogs, and fish. The smell of the food turned Tourvanda's stomach. She was not familiar with these American dishes and only ate an apple and a piece of bread. Arpi and Seta chattered about their life in Italy. Tourvanda remained silent and listened with only passive interest.

After dinner she accompanied them up the grand staircase, where the noise from the Hall followed her from the second floor. Tourvanda's room was the first one on the right on the third floor. It had three or four single beds, a toilet and a sink, and she was the only inhabitant that evening. In the past Tourvanda was accustomed to going to bed early. This night was no exception. On subsequent days immigrant girls came and left. Every night an attendant locked the door.

The next morning she walked over to the railing alongside the balcony that circled the Great Hall in the Immigration Processing Area, and looked down at the ballroom-like space of immigrants milling about looking like a hive of frantic bees—a tapestry of color and sound. Peasant red and green glared against a blur of widow's black. The room buzzed with foreign words, officials shouting instructions, muttered prayers and fragments of tunes hummed in native tongues. Every few moments a voice bellowed a name over the loudspeaker, answered with shouts of joy from those accepted and soft wails from those still waiting. The chaos of sights and sounds below made Tourvanda's heart race.

The affluent newcomers had brought family heir-looms on the long journey across the ocean. Checkered cloths covered baskets of family treasures which often included a month's supply of food, antiques, quilts and small Oriental rugs. Those less well-to-do carried only their hats or purses.

Tourvanda's mind drifted. Memories of her depar-ture from Egypt came back; a girlfriend's final wish for Tourvanda to find her a husband brought a smile still vivid in her imagination. She told her, "My cousin Harry say handsome men in America looking for wife, I find you a rich one." Her friends had laughed. It had been a happy day, full of promise. Going to her cousins in America symbolized hope, optimism and a break from the past.

Tourvanda was twenty years old. Her body was lean; she had her mother's shapely legs, and a light complexion that contrasted her dark hair and vacant eyes. Her wish was to live with her relatives in New York. If they sent her back to Egypt, she'd return to strangers.

The rush of people in the hallway brought her back to reality. She joined the stream of people pushing and shoving to the top of the wide staircase. She clutched the banister with a sense of urgency and slowly walked down the stairs worn thin by the feet of thousands of immigrants who had passed through this Great Hall. An immigration authority walked toward her. She stared at the floor, bracing herself for bad news. The click of the officer's heels passed by her solitary figure; Tourvanda let out a shivery breath.

She walked over to the Great Hall, sat on a bench and waited for her name to be called over the Public Address system. This was a daily ritual for two months. The officials never explained why she was detained for so long, but other immigrants suggested something might have been wrong with her credentials. Tourvanda thought that it was because she was here on a visitor's pass and the officials thought that she might not return to Egypt willingly.

When she walked up the stairs one afternoon she passed Arpi and Seta's room and heard muffled sobs. She knocked. There was a choked, feeble, "Come in." The two girls cried out, "They're sending us back to Italy, Tourvanda." She nervously looked at the girls, attempting to hide her own sudden anxiety.

"Tourvanda," the older girl cried, "will they send you back to Old Country, like they send us?"

Tourvanda shrugged. "Officials send you back because your brother in America is not a citizen. I am here on six months visa to visit cousins Harry and Dick. They will find a way for me to stay."

Arpi stopped crying long enough to say, "But don't you see? Your cousins are not citizens either. They will send you back, too."

"Iss possible." Tourvanda moved toward the door and glanced back at the two girls lamenting their fate. "Goodbye," she whispered, closing the door on their sobs. She hurried back to her room and closed the door, trying to muffle her cries with her pillow. "I can't go back," she wept. "Please God, I can't go back to strangers."

Arpi and Seta had gone but strangely Tourvanda remained. Her life had already assumed a strange regularity within the confine of Ellis Island. After three weeks, Cousin Harry was allowed to visit for one hour. It was a hardship for him, as it meant a six hour train ride from his work in Lake George. It was, however, a comfort for Tourvanda.

Three weeks later, the other remaining Ahigian relatives visited. The tall, lanky, nearly bald Armenian with a thin mustache introduced himself as Cousin Dick. At his side was a dark haired, light-skinned, short woman who was his wife. The last time the two cousins had been together, Tourvanda was an infant in Palanga, Western Armenia. For a brief moment, Tourvanda's euphoria first experienced on the day she arrived had returned. The two relatives exchanged joyful exultation. Zevart, Cousin Dick's wife, presented her with a lovely blue dress with beautiful paisley prints. Cousin Dick motioned for them to sit on one of the long wooden benches in the Great Hall. Talk became serious.

"If they send you back," Cousin Dick said, "don't worry. We write letters and send you packages. We keep in touch. You are not alone now."

Zevart held Tourvanda's hand firmly and said, "Now you know you have a family. Don't worry."

Tourvanda found little comfort in their words. She knew they could never relate to her potential reality of returning to loneliness.

The monotonous routine of waiting continued. At one point she encountered an official who informed her that a ship was departing for Egypt and that she would leave Ellis Island in one week. She ran to her room and wept.

When Cousin Harry came for another visit the following day, she mustered her courage to tell him. "They're going to send me back to Egypt in one week." The tears streamed down her cheeks.

Cousin Harry put his arm around her. "Tourvanda, you must understand that the immigration rules cannot be changed or appealed. If they send you back, there's nothing more we can do."

"You don't understand, Cousin Harry," she cried. "I have lived with strangers all my life. I have waited years to find you and now I must go back to strangers again." Cousin Harry hugged and kissed her, tried to comfort her and left.

For one week Tourvanda wept and worried. On the last day the authorities took her and another Armenian girl and put them in the hull of a steamer. Thirty minutes later voices and footsteps approached. An official unlocked the door and a lawyer took both the girls and walked them back to the ferry. They followed obediently, afraid to ask questions. They had no idea why they were being taken off the ship, but Tourvanda thought perhaps there might be a possibility she could stay in America.

There was a resumption of life in seclusion on Ellis Island for two more weeks. There was again no explanation for these events. She went daily to breakfast, but had no appetite. She sat in her usual spot in the Great Hall and played solitaire, read books or *The Hairenik*, an Armenian newspaper. One morning a voice over the loudspeaker crackled, "Tourvanda Ahigian, Yovich Platz, Maria Ciucci, Ivan Alexander and Vincent Meier."

An interpreter walked over to them and said they could leave Ellis Island today. The lady instructed the

immigrants to gather at the gate, where they could telegram relatives of their arrival. Tourvanda sent joyful word
to Cousin Harry.

The official asked Tourvanda for a dollar and handed
her a ham sandwich in a brown paper bag. The lady
pinned a name tag on her dress: Tourvanda Ahigian.
Watervliet, New York. Those immigrants still waiting
crowded about her cheering her good fortune, carrying her
suitcase and wishing her well.

On a cloudless May afternoon in 1928, an official
escorted her through the front doors of the Immigration
Building into the sunshine. She watched the gulls swoop
overhead.

"I'm out of my cage," she whispered to herself. "Now
I can be free like these birds." She took a deep breath of
the crisp air. "Where do I go now, sir?"

"Follow me," said the official. He guided her past
rows of budding spring trees onto the ferry to Battery Park,
and from there to a train heading upstate. The official bid
her a pleasant journey and left.

Tourvanda took a seat next to a window, extended
her palms heavenward and cried, "Park Asdoozoh," giving
thanks to God. As the train began to move she looked out
the window, which framed the view like paintings in an art
museum. The trees were blossoming in the New York
countryside and along the winding Hudson River. She saw
a farmer plowing his field, which brought memories of
childhood when her late cousin Mergiditch would passionately plant his vegetable garden.

For the first time in two months Tourvanda's appetite had returned. She unwrapped and devoured the ham
sandwich she had bought on Ellis Island. It was the first
time she had tasted ham; pigs were considered unclean
animals in the Old Country. Impatiently, she listened and
waited to hear the conductor call Watervliet, New York.
The distance was unknown. At each stop came the
thought that maybe it was her turn to exit. It stopped at so
many places and crowds got on and off; a draining experience. She leaned back on the padded head cushion to rest
but could not sleep. The movement of the train, and the
clackety-clack of the iron wheels reminded her of a train
ride in Egypt when she had gone to a resort by the ocean

for a week. Even though Egypt was a beautiful country, she had no family or close friends there.

At ten o'clock that evening, the conductor called out, "Watervliet, next stop." He put his hand on Tourvanda's shoulder and said, "You get off here, young lady."

*   *   *   *

She grabbed her suitcase and was the first one to step down onto the depot platform when the train stopped. A single street light illuminated the area. She glanced up and down the landing and saw only a few strangers waiting to greet passengers. Neither Dick nor Harry was in sight. The other passengers and friends departed, leaving no one. She glanced at the sign on the side of the depot: *WATERVLIET.* The letters matched her name tag.

"No, I'm in right place. Maybe train is early and they're not here yet. I wait."

Tourvanda walked over to a long bench outside the depot and sat down, placing the suitcase on her lap. She shivered in the damp night air and wished for a coat or shawl. "At least it isn't as cold as the March days on Ellis Island," she thought to herself. Officials there had herded the detained immigrants outdoors daily for exercise whether they had coats or not.

Suddenly she heard a voice calling, "Tourvanda! Tourvanda! Here we are!." The attractive wife of Cousin Dick came toward her with a little boy at her heels.

"Zevart, I thought Cousin Harry would be here to meet me. I am glad to see you. I wait and worry if anybody coming to get me."

Out of breath, Zevart gasped, "Cousin Harry had to go to Lake George to work and will return on the weekend. Dick and I came to meet you. There are two train depots in Watervliet, we weren't sure which one your train would stop at, so we split up. Dick and his friend, Harry Avakian, are waiting at the other depot. I'm sorry we worried you."

"Iss all right. You here now."

"This is my son, Harry Junior. A neighbor is home watching Gerald, our five-year-old, and Harry's daughter, Helen.

Tourvanda looked at Harry Jr. "Hello, I am cousin Tourvanda."

Harry nodded and stared at the ground.

Zevart patted her son on the head. "Carry the suitcase for your cousin, Junior."

Tourvanda was possessive of the suitcase. "No, no," she said, "I do myself." She held onto the handle firmly. "How far we go?"

"Just a few blocks. Follow me. Dick and his neighbor Harry Avakian are probably there waiting by now."

They walked three blocks on a gravel road, past a row of white framed houses set close together. A few puddles remained from a recent rain. Harry Jr. avoided the puddles at first, but couldn't resist jumping in one while Zevart was busy talking. He splashed the ladies' skirts and his mother gave him a swat on the bottom.

"I'm sorry, Tourvanda," Zevart said, trying to wipe the muddy spots off her visitor's skirt.

"Iss all right," Tourvanda replied. "This boy's a handful," she muttered to herself.

As they were walking, Tourvanda remembered Zevart's letter she had received in Alexandria. "Remember you said when I got to America, we could go places together? Remember that picture you sent me of Cousin Dick, you and Harry Jr.?"

"Yes, I remember."

"I still have that letter and picture with me in my suitcase. It meant a lot to me."

As they neared the Ahigian flat, Tourvanda saw Dick and Harry Avakian on the porch.

"My Tourvanda," Cousin Dick called out and came running down the steps to embrace her. "You were only a little baby when I saw you last. You've become quite a beautiful woman since." He smiled and turned to Harry. "Harry here iss good friend. He and wife Margaret live down the street."

"You pretty girl, Tourvanda." Harry grinned. "Won't have trouble finding husband soon."

Tourvanda frowned at the unwelcome suggestion and thought, "I don't want husband, just my cousins."

"My wife, Margaret, would like to meet you," Harry said. *"Quiche air pahree,* goodnight." He waved and left, heading down the sidewalk. Dick took Tourvanda's arm in his and led her inside to her new home.

Chapter 2

Cousin Dick thanked the neighbor for watching the younger children, who were sound asleep. When the neighbor had gone, Cousin Dick took Tourvanda's hand and led her through the house. "I show you where you sleep." He pointed to a small storage space off the dining room with a mattress set on the frame of a wooden box. "I'm sorry, you'll have to share this bed with our five-year-old son, Gerald."

"Doesn't matter. I'm used to sleeping on the ground. I don't want to bother him."

"He is sound sleeper. Let's talk some." Dick motioned for her to join him in the kitchen where Zevart was already waiting, with a cup of coffee held firmly in both hands. The three sat talking of Cousin Dick's past and current life in New York. Tourvanda learned quickly that he enjoyed storytelling, especially when it came to relating his own exploits. He had worked in a factory which sold steel to industrial businesses to make equipment, having spent his last five years enduring the six a.m. to five p.m. shift. His main objective when he came to the United States eighteen years before had been to raise enough money to return and support his Armenian relatives in the Old Country.

When speaking of his life in New York, Cousin Dick was very animated, yet at the same time full of pride. Tourvanda and Zevart endured nearly two hours of stories relating to factory occurrences, domestic livings, holidays and various other episodes involving the clash of Armenian and American cultures which, according to Cousin Dick, were numerous. He told these anecdotes with a smile to show he was not always taking himself seriously.

Unfortunately, he did not pick up on Zevart's and Tourvanda's boredom, which had increased to a point where they had nearly fallen asleep. At the end of this one-sided dialogue, Cousin Dick asked suddenly, "Do you know why officials let you go from Ellis Island?"

Tourvanda shook her head. "Do you know?"

"A week ago our priest wrote a letter on your behalf saying we would sponsor you and that we had stable jobs. We paid him five hundred dollars, which we borrowed from Harry Avakian's cousin, to buy you a United States government bond to assure the government that should something happen, you will not become a burden."

Tourvanda shook her head. "I'm too much problem for you."

"No, no. You are an Ahigian. We do anything for you." He stood and walked to the stove to fill a cup with Zevart's coffee. "I hope you don't mind being alone with Gerald until the other children get home from school at three. Harry, Zevart, and I work during the day and usually get back around five."

In a tone that revealed great enthusiasm Tourvanda asked, "Can I go to school, too? I want to learn to better read and write English. So much to learn."

Dick raised an eyebrow. "Maybe possible. I call school tomorrow and find out."

"All my life I want to learn."

"Don't get your hopes too high, you might be too old for this school."

"Then I keep busy. Will cook and clean for you."

Zevart cleared her throat and interrupted. "No, no, that's not necessary. I do that."

Tourvanda flushed. "Then I will care for children after school."

Cousin Dick looked to Zevart and both nodded. With that settled, the relatives said goodnight. Tourvanda walked to her bed where little Gerald lay in quiet slumber. The space was cramped, in keeping with the rest of the small, five-room flat. Cousin Harry, who was away at Lake George, and his six-year-old daughter, Helen, slept in one bedroom; Cousin Dick, Zevart and their six-year-old son, Harry Jr., slept in the other.

The following day Tourvanda dusted, cleaned and watched over Gerald. All the while she took in the numerous details of her new surroundings.

The flat's kitchen, parlor, dining room and bathroom spaces were all limited, yet kept spotless. Tourvanda learned that the parlor and dining room were used only on high holidays. All socializing took place in the kitchen, which was furnished with a maroon velvet sofa, a white enamel-topped table and four wooden chairs. The old-fashioned gas stove was used for cooking and heating the house.

Dick called the school the next day and was told that Tourvanda couldn't attend at the elementary level, but classes for adults were scheduled to begin within a few months. The principal promised to let Dick know when and where the classes would be held.

After Tourvanda was settled a few weeks later, her cousins hosted a welcoming party. Armenian neighbors were invited to see the new arrival from the Old Country. Cousin Dick was delighted to have visitors in his home, as he had never hosted so many friends at once and it allowed a greater audience for his storytelling. Everyone congregated in the kitchen where Zevart brought Tourvanda's suitcase, opened it, and showed her guests how neatly everything had been packed, showcasing the needlework Tourvanda learned in Egypt.

Rose, an Armenian who lived downstairs, added, "Tourvanda, you're a wonderful seamstress. Why don't you get a job sewing?"

Tourvanda shrugged and said maybe.

Another neighbor, Lucy, said, "Why don't you change your name to something that sounds more American, like maybe Victoria or Veronica or something?"

"Oh...do you think I could?" Her voice rose two octaves higher. "I never liked my name."

"Sure, come on, let's take a vote." Rose didn't wait for an answer. She called for attention. "Raise your hand if you think Tourvanda should change her name."

It was unanimous. Amid much laughter and gaiety, Tourvanda announced, "Okay. Now I'm real American. From this time on I change my name to Victoria."

Over the next several months Victoria hardly left the flat. A new routine began which consisted of washing dishes, dusting, cleaning and being careful not to infringe on Zevart's domain. She frequently read *The Hairenik*, which kept in tune with happenings in the Old Country and also kept her in touch with the language, which had been sifted out of her vocabulary while becoming acquainted with the American culture and tradition. Life in America wasn't what she expected. Her cousins were gone most of the day working, often times leaving her lonely. Her spirits would rise when the children arrived from school; they kept her occupied in the afternoon with various toys and games. Evenings were spent listening to Cousin Dick's stories and his violin. After several weeks with little to do she would often go to bed early. Soon came the realization that she was totally dependent on her cousins for food and shelter, a few clothes and personal necessities. Cousin Dick infrequently gave her an allowance of one dollar, which she kept in a handkerchief stored in her suitcase.

Seven months later, money was scarce for household expenses and Christmas was coming. Harry bluntly suggested she find work...Harry Jr. could watch over the younger children as he had before she arrived.

Victoria slept little that night. Her thoughts focused on Cousin Harry. She knew it had been hard for him to ask her to work; it meant there was not enough money. She wanted to help the family, yet was equally concerned that jobs would be scarce for those like her who had no skills. Further, there was no way of her getting around as no one had a car and she was still unfamiliar with public transportation and the area around Watervliet. There was the remembrance of the neighbor, Rose, who had suggested she find a job sewing. Victoria recalled that Zevart had once mentioned a coat factory a few blocks away which often employed women seamstresses. With cautious enthusiasm she resolved to visit the coat factory the following day and see if she might obtain a job.

After lunch the next day, Victoria borrowed a sweater from Zevart and walked two blocks in the snow without galoshes to the overcoat factory. She approached the man in the front office and said, "I want a job."

His brown, bloodshot eyes peered through thick glasses. "Can you sew?"

She nodded. "Sew good. Work hard."

"You new to this country? Where you from?"

"Armenia."

"Good workers." He nodded. "We have some. I'm Abe Kaplan, the boss." He stood without offering his hand to shake. "Follow me."

Abe Kaplan led the way up a narrow staircase to the second floor. The racket of sewing machines hit Victoria's ears like swarming bees, the smell of cloth and oil permeated the room.

The boss pointed to an empty stool and the woman sitting next to it. "This is Anna. She's Armenian, too. Been working here five years already. You sit here and baste collars and cuffs for overcoats. Anna will show you what to do."

Victoria worked beside Anna. She learned quickly to baste the collars and cuffs; within a short while she was nearly as good as Anna and just as efficient. However, because she hadn't sewn since being at Ellis Island, her fingers quickly became sore from shoving the needle through thick layers of fabric.

At five the bell rang as the workers organized their stations and then scattered. Victoria ran home, unaware of the cold, too excited with the recognition that she now had a job. She would be paid to sew, something which she enjoyed. There would no longer be the feeling of indebtedness steeped with guilt toward her cousins; there would be a new, fourth source of income. She would no longer spend her days in solitude. There were now Armenian friends with whom she could regularly speak her native language.

When Dick and Zevart got home from work, Victoria announced proudly, "I have a job." Zevart was speechless. Dick ran to her. "That's good news. Now, with real job, you are one hundred percent American. This calls for a toast." He hugged her and then went to the cupboard and grabbed a bottle of wine, which was reserved for only special occurrences. "Good luck, Victoria, on you new job." He poured wine for the three of them and together they cheered her good fortune.

At the end of the first week Victoria received her first pay—twelve dollars cash in a small brown envelope. When Cousin Harry returned from Lake George for the weekend, he took her shopping to buy a winter coat and galoshes. He also helped her pick out a dark green dress to wear to work, and a pair of sturdy walking shoes. She finally had something to wear besides the blue dress that Zevart had given her while she was at Ellis Island, which from constant use was worn and faded.

Victoria and Anna ate lunch together regularly, talking about work and their families. Eventually, Anna confided details of her unhappy marriage. "I did not choose my husband, Levon. When we lived in Armenia my parents arranged marriage with a friend's son who lived in America. Older than me but had good job and needed a wife."

"Did you meet him before the wedding?"

"Only pictures. But I wanted to come to America and this was my only way. A lot of my Armenian girlfriends came to America as mail-order brides."

"Why you unhappy with husband?"

"Armenian couples usually move in with husband's family. Levon's mother give me trouble all the time. She's mean, jealous woman and Levon always take her side. Sometimes they get mad and both don't speak to me for days." Tears came to Anna's eyes. "Be careful, Victoria. Listen to me. Don't marry a stranger."

Victoria frowned. "I won't, don't worry. I don't want marriage to anybody."

The following Saturday Victoria returned home from work to see Harry Avakian and her cousin Dick talking to a visitor in the living room.

The men stood up as she walked in. "Hello, Victoria," said Dick, smiling. "Come sit down."

She sat in a chair in a corner, withdrawn from the men.

"Victoria," Harry Avakian began, "I'd like you to meet my cousin, Michael Haroutunian, from Michigan."

She nodded.

Harry went on. "Your cousin Dick was telling us how happy you are to be in America."

Victoria kept her eyes on the carpet, rather timid to be in the company of two strangers, and said, "Yes."

Cousin Dick turned to Harry Avakian and said, "Let's go out to the kitchen. I want to show you my old violin."

They left her alone in the parlor with the strange man, who sat down on a sofa opposite her. He wore a gray suit with a silk paisley scarf around his neck, and black shoes buffed to a shine. A short, slim man, he had hazel eyes, dark brown hair, a light complexion, and a prominent nose.

Michael looked at her shyly and smiled. "Your cousin Dick told me you had a problem getting into America. He said you stayed in orphanages in the Old Country. Which ones were you in?"

"Kharpet, Mezreh, and in many other different countries."

"Kharpet! I stayed at that orphanage, too. Once I ran away to my cousin Lucintac's village to get food without permission. When they caught me, they wouldn't let me back in the orphanage. When were you there?"

"1918. Where do you live now?"

"I live in Pontiac, Michigan with my two brothers. Harry Avakian is my cousin, one of my favorites." He went on to talk of Harry Avakian for nearly an hour.

When it was time to leave, Michael smiled and said, "I enjoyed our visit today, Victoria. Goodnight."

"Goodnight." She smiled to herself thinking he wasn't a bad-looking man. He had smiled often, showing the straightest, whitest teeth. But he was too short, too round-shouldered.

Michael returned for another visit the next day, and again he and Victoria were alone in the parlor. He sat next to her, his hat clutched between two shaking hands. He wasted no time in getting to his purpose. "I have three weeks' leave of absence from work. You don't know me, so I tell you. I am twenty-seven years old, have good, steady work at Wilson Foundry in Michigan. We melt down steel for cars and I make forty dollars a week."

Victoria's eyes widened in awe.

"I live with my brother, Armen, and we bought a new car, a beige Whippet. I have eighteen hundred dollar savings, a one hundred dollar life insurance policy, and I am healthy. Strong stock." He smiled at her proudly, his hands busy turning his hat. "You and I have much in common and I think we could be happy together." Looking first to his left out a window and slowly moving his gaze back to her, he bit his lip and paused. "Will you marry me, Victoria?"

She stared at him, rolled her eyes, and shook her head. "No, I don't want to marry."

"Why not?" Frustrated.

"I just found my cousins and I don't want to live in Michigan, so far away."

"You can come back for a visit every year, I promise."

"No. Iss impossible. No."

Michael stood up, still clutching his hat. "Please think about it. You want to stay here with your cousins forever, or have your own place? Think about how we can build future together. Have our own family. I come back tomorrow to visit...we talk some more."

After Michael left, Victoria sat twirling her thumbs as she often did when she was nervous, and considered Michael's proposal. Her job gave her precious independence, income, and a good friend. She had developed a strong attachment to her cousins and she felt that that was her family. Still, it was Zevart's home. She could not remain there indefinitely, yet Anna's words of warning flashed through her mind: Do not marry a stranger. It sounded as if Michael would be a good provider, with a car and money in the bank. And he promised she could come back for a visit every year.

The following evening, Michael paid another call to Victoria, holding a bouquet of roses.

She blushed, shaking her head and avoiding his eyes. "Iss pretty, but cost too much. Flowers don't last."

"They show how much I like you," he said with a big smile.

Victoria sat on the sofa and Michael sat down beside her. "I tell you a funny story," he said cheerfully. He jumped back to his feet, paced the room, arms waving. "My brother Louis and I were coming to America on a Greek ship and another passenger told us if we hear the horn blowing a lot it mean danger and we should grab a life preserver and jump overboard."

Victoria sat rigid, back against the sofa, eyes following Michael's movements closely. She did not quite understand the relevance of his story.

"One night we were sleeping and the horn blow so loud it wake us up. My brother and I grab a life preserver and run up on deck. I climb up on the railing and just as I was going to jump in ocean, a Greek man pull me back, shouting, 'Stop. Don't jump!'

"'Let go!' I yell at him. 'That horn means danger. We must jump.'

"He laugh at me. 'No danger. Ships talk to each other that way. The big horn is saying hello.'" Michael sat down again, grinning at Victoria. "Isn't that funny story? I almost jump in sea for nothing."

Victoria smiled. "On my trip here I see sharks racing with the ship. With great big mouths and sharp teeth. You would have been a good dinner."

Michael laughed. "Good thing I don't jump. You wouldn't have flowers today."

Victoria felt a little more comfortable with this humorous, impulsive, interloper. Still, after he left, she was even more confused. Was it possible to have affection for a man she had only known for three days? He was a good-looking, cheerful and smart man, but Victoria harbored the romantic notion that if she'd ever marry it would be to a man to whom she was entirely, unquestionably devoted. She also imagined him to be a tall and handsome suitor. Love was supposed to be a great overwhelming emotion. Here she felt little except the cold reality that she could not indefinitely remain with her cousins. Further, she had never before been an object of a man's heart's desire. There was no comfort in the knowledge that she had little choice in the matter.

During his next visit, Michael said, "Have you made decision yet, Victoria? I must know right away. If answer yes, I must get your cousin's permission. We only have two weeks left for engagement party and wedding. Will you marry me, yes or no?"

Victoria sat studying her twirling thumbs. "I can't manage a house." She shook her head. "Don't know how to cook. Be terrible wife."

"You smart, you learn fast.   Every woman makes good wife with practice."

Victoria leaned back against the sofa, weary and drained of her resolve not to marry.   She knew her presence crowded her cousins...strained their budget.

"Yes."

Chapter 3

Two days later Victoria was sitting at the kitchen table crying. Cousin Harry found her there on his way out to work. He asked hurriedly, "What's the matter, *Jahdu*?" (sweet child)

"School principal call today. He say they going to start classes for grown-up people to learn English. I want to go to school, not get married."

Harry shook his head. "Don't cry. Look at all the girls who want a husband and can't find one. Be happy someone wants to marry you. You'll get used to Michael, he is good man."

Victoria shook her head, unsatisfied.

The following Saturday night, cousin Zevart prepared a special dinner for the formal Armenian engagement. A priest performed the liturgy, a tradition in the Armenian culture. Michael and Victoria stood side-by-side while prayers and chants were read and sung from the Armenian Bible. The priest raised his cross, wrapped in a lace cloth, and blessed the new couple. Good luck favors of white candied almonds, wrapped in netting and tied with a ribbon, were passed out to the single girls.

The next ten days were busy with preparation for the wedding. Cousin Dick asked Michael to repay the five hundred dollars borrowed from Harry Avakian's cousin for the government bond that allowed Victoria to remain in the United States. Michael also gave Harry's wife, Margaret, money for the wedding ring, bridal gown, church and reception expenses. His savings were depleted to less than one hundred dollars. On February 24, 1929, a visiting Archbishop from Egypt married Michael and Victoria in the Armenian Church of Troy, New York.

After the service, the wedding guests found their cars and formed a motorcade to the Avakian home in Watervliet, where a lavish reception awaited them. A chorus of horns sounded throughout the trip back. When they reached the Avakian home, Margaret led the wedding party into the house, waving a white lace handkerchief and dancing to Armenian bridal music. One of Harry Avakian's cousins played the *zoornah* to a high, raspy, festive melody which ushered the bride and groom into the house. The bridal party formed a human chain linked by each other's fingers and danced into the house behind the wedding pair, as was the custom in Old Armenia.

The *keyknee* (wine), was passed to everyone as the best man, Harry Avakian, offered a toast to the bride and groom. "Here's to a good life together for Michael and Victoria. May you grow old on one pillow."

Platters and bowls of food covered the table. Pungent aromas made stomachs growl as the guests lined up for stuffed grape leaves, dried spiced beef and pickled vegetables, meatballs and chicken, pilaf and pita bread.

Of the fifty guests, Victoria recognized a face in the crowd—Zadig Garabedian, her first Armenian school teacher from her village of Palanga in Turkish Armenia. She felt strange to see him after so many years. He settled in Watervliet after he arrived in America.

The celebration lasted until eleven o'clock that night. After many of the guests had departed, Michael changed his clothes at Margaret's, while Victoria preferred to change at Cousin Dick's. She rejoined Michael at the Avakians where she said a tearful farewell to her cousins and well-wishers still remaining from the party. Harry Avakian then gathered the newlyweds and drove them to the Albany rail-road station, where they would catch a train to Michigan.

The Pullman Express, which would take them to their new home, included sleeping coaches. They found theirs and Michael ushered Victoria inside. He set the luggage at the foot of their berth and they stood before each other in an uneasy silence. Michael glanced at her as he began to remove his clothes and fold them neatly; Victoria watched with embarrassment as he removed his shirt and trousers, revealing long johns. She felt her face grow warm. "I can't do this," she thought wildly. "I can't get undressed in front of a man."

Michael said, with a laugh which eased the growing tension, "We can set our clothes on the bags. I'll sleep in my underwear. We're tired, Victoria. We just sleep tonight."

She closed her eyes and gave thanks to God. Removing her dress, Victoria folded it with some effort and placed it on top of Michael's clothes. Wearing a white silk slip, she crawled under the covers and turned toward the window, back to her husband.

"Goodnight, Victoria," Michael said softly.

She laid awake long after Michael slept.

Years later Victoria found out that on the first day she arrived on the train, Harry Avakian had suggested to Cousin Dick matchmaking her with his cousin Michael. Cousin Dick agreed and Harry Avakian sent a telegram to Michael:

"Lovely Armenian orphan here.
Come quickly to marry!
Harry."

Michael had taken a three week leave of absence from his job, pocketed his eighteen hundred dollar savings, and left by train for Watervliet.

The bride and groom moved into Michael's brother Armen's house in Pontiac, taking one of three bedrooms upstairs. A third brother, Louis, occupied the second room, the third was vacant. Armen and his wife and their three year old son, Vartkes, slept in another bedroom on the first floor. The house was more comfortable than Watervliet: the double bed had an iron frame and a mattress with new springs. Only Michael shared her room. The house itself was two storeys with the three small bedrooms and a bath upstairs; kitchen, dining room, parlor and bedroom downstairs.

Every week during the first month, Armenian relatives and friends came to meet the new bride. Drinks, appetizers, chicken, pilaf and Armenian pastries were served. The merry-making included Armen's wife Gladys playing the oud, a medieval belly-shaped stringed instrument. Michael played the tambourine, Louis the mandolin, and Armen sang the old Armenian folk songs. The others clapped hands in rhythm to the tambourine and danced in a circle, enjoying the familiar customs that gave their lives continuity. The buffet table filled with Armenian delicacies made Victoria feel uneasy as flashbacks of her hungry days in the orphanage crowded her mind.

Victoria would watch the festivities with interest. She had never before heard Armenian music or watched their dances. The American Near East missionaries who had looked after her were unfamiliar with any Armenian cultural activities and therefore never encouraged any.

At one party Michael rushed with hands extended to his withdrawn wife. "Come, Victoria, the bride and groom should lead the dance."

"No, I don't dance." Victoria folded her arms, frowned, and said quietly, "Leave me alone, please."

His face flushed and he turned away. Victoria watched the women laughing, eyes sparkling, hands clapping, and thought glumly that they were celebrating her marriage while she sat alone. They are happy, but not me. I would rather be in Watervliet with my cousins, and go to school so that I can learn English instead of being here with all these strangers we have to pay to feed.

After the guests said goodnight, Victoria helped clean. Michael was in celebratory spirits. "I think everyone had a great time, don't you?"

"Too much noise and people for me. Work and expense for nothing."

Michael's mood sank. "Huh! I didn't know you were such an unsociable person. You don't like having fun, do you? Well, you can relax now...the month of welcoming parties is over."

"Good," she responded.

*   *   *   *

Two weeks later Armen's wife Gladys gave birth to Vartouhi, named after Armen's mother. Victoria took over the household chores, washing dishes, dusting and cleaning as she had for her cousins. A new and yet all too familiar routine was starting to settle.

One morning, Armen said, "I have a taste for meatball soup, Victoria. There's hamburger, eggs, flour, onions and rice in the ice box and cupboard. Will you make some for dinner tonight?"

"I will try," she replied. To herself she thought, I haven't any idea how to make meatball soup. Or anything else, for that matter. I been a servant girl but never had to cook, just clean and care for children. He'll be sorry he ask me to cook. She worked on the soup for hours, ashamed to ask Gladys for advice. The meatballs were a soggy mess. At dinner no one cracked a smile or complained, but politely finished the meal. Consequently, Gladys began to teach Victoria how to cook.

Victoria washed clothes and diapers on the metal scrubboard, scraping the skin off her fingers in the process. When little Vartouhi was three weeks old, Armen had a new washing machine delivered and installed in the basement. Victoria couldn't believe her eyes.

Armen grinned. "There you are, Victoria. In America there is easy way to wash. Now you don't have to scrub all those diapers on a board. This will save you lot of work." He headed toward the stairs. "You do first wash now while I'm having lunch."

She stared at the monolithic machine. "What do I do with this thing?" she grumbled. "How do I turn it on? Armen should have showed me. I hate this machine...iss better old way. Get clothes cleaner for cheaper. I do it my way. Always they want me to change, be different. My way iss better." She shook her head and attempted to use the machine, but a few minutes later her attempts met with great pain. She let out a loud scream, which brought Armen downstairs yelling, "What wrong? Victoria! What happen?"

"Help! My hair caught!" Her head was pulled close to the machine and being dragged closer.

"Wait..." Armen yelled. "Don't move." He rushed to her side and stopped the machine, then hit the release lever on the wringer. He unwound her hair from the rolls and held the sobbing girl until she composed herself. "There now, you okay?"

Victoria frowned. "I like the old way to wash clothes better." She put her hand to her head, feeling uneven chopped hair.

"Wait till you learn machine. You will like it. Save you much work."

*   *   *   *

Spring days arrived with robins, shirtsleeves, grass to cut, picnics and rides in the country. Michael and Armen shared ownership of the beige Whippet, used mainly to shop for groceries and visiting relatives in Detroit. On Saturdays, after supper, Michael would take Victoria for a ride. On one such evening Michael was especially eager to drive.

"Finished with the dishes, *Anush* (sweet one)?" Michael asked.

"I don't like sweet talk," she responded, shrinking from the endearment. "Yes, I'm done."

Michael went out to start the car. Victoria followed after a few minutes, bundled in a sweater and headscarf. "Where we go today?"

"Back to Walled Lake Casino. Iss nice to listen to the music and look at water."

A half hour later Michael parked the Whippet by the edge of the lake, not far from the Casino. A dance band was playing. Victoria was amazed how Americans always found time for enjoyment. For several minutes they sat listening to the music, which enhanced the already tranquil surrounding, and watched dusk settle over the water. Lights flickered across the lake and a few seagulls swooped toward the water, cawing.

"It amazes me," Michael said softly, "how birds survive. It says in the Bible, 'Look at the birds in the heavens. They neither sow nor reap; yet God feeds them.'" Michael watched for a moment.

"When I walked out of Ellis Island, I felt like those birds. It was the happiest day for me. Leaving Ellis Island I felt like I could finally survive on my own."

"You don't talk about your past, Victoria. Tell me about your life in the Old Country."

She shook her head and began to twirl her thumbs. "Too long. Too complicated. Not now."

Michael sighed. "All right. Maybe someday you will feel comfortable enough to tell me."

She focused the talk toward his past. "Tell me how you come to America. Are you citizen?"

"My brother Armen came over here in 1913 to avoid draft in Old Country. Then he help Louis and me come to America, but it was illegal way. He had no choice. He bribed the bus driver to let us lie under the bus seats as we went through Canadian customs into the States."

"You are here illegal? Aren't you afraid they send you back to Turkish Armenia?" Victoria shivered, for she well remembered the fear of being sent back; it was still present in her mind.

"I try not to think about it. Are you citizen?"

"No. But I come through Ellis Island, so I must be legal."

Michael nodded.

"We better get back. Armen will worry."

Michael started the Whippet and they rode home in silence.

Chapter 4

A month later Victoria realized she was pregnant. Instead of feeling proud and happy she was ashamed, shy and embarrassed to the point where she told no one. Back in the Old Country no one ever openly acknowledged pregnancies, as the topic of how babies were made was a "dirty" subject which honest religious folk did not discuss. Eventually, however, Victoria's changing body revealed her condition, which brought great pride and happiness to Michael, who hoped that they might have a dozen children together.

All across the country the economy worsened with thousands of men being laid off. Wilson Foundry had announced plans to consolidate operations due to heavy financial losses. Victoria and Michael were concerned that his lack of seniority would mean he might be one of the first to go. Matters were complicated with most of the savings having been spent for the wedding while expenses continued to increase. The possibility of having another mouth to feed with limited resources was a grim glimpse of future reality.

Much of the United States was preoccupied with the plummeting economy, which hit an all time low with the historic stock market crash of October 29, 1929. Panicking businesses were taking severe measures to avoid heavy financial losses, measures which often included drastic layoffs. In November of that same year Wilson Foundry began sending notices to many, saying that their services were no longer needed. Michael received one such notice, which promised that he would be recalled immediately should the situation change.

On December 13th their son Johnny was born. What should have been a joyful event was filled with complications. Johnny was born with a narrow esophagus and was therefore unable to swallow fluids. His doctor, Dr. Castell, was summoned. He carefully examined the infant and insisted that milk and oatmeal would heal him, but Johnny only vomited this prescription, losing three pounds in two weeks and thus taking on the frightful appearance of a shrunken prune. Michael and Victoria feared the worst, as neither understood the baby's ailment nor the complex medical terms Dr. Castell used to explain. As Johnny's condition worsened, a neighbor suggested taking him to the hospital where a specialist named Dr. Geralds might be able to help. Desperate, they agreed and checked into the hospital, where Johnny was kept separated from Victoria; she and Michael kept quiet vigil for several days outside the nursery waiting for word of his health. Dr. Geralds came at their request to observe the baby and after two days agreed to perform a complex surgery which required Michael to give blood for a transfusion.

After several hours of tense and anxious waiting, Michael and Victoria learned that Johnny would recover and likely live a normal, healthy life. The relieved parents were allowed to see their son shortly after surgery; he was released from the hospital a month later after showing definite signs of weight gain.

Michael agreed to perform two years of manual labor for the two doctors in order to pay off the five hundred dollar fee that went with the surgery.

In 1932 economic conditions had not improved. With no income, Michael was unable to pay Armen his half of the rent and the car payments. He relinquished his share of the Whippet and moved his family to an empty room at cousin Melkon's house. After two months life had not improved. Michael's debts increased daily and he was still unable to pay his rent. Not wishing to be a financial burden on anyone and against the wishes of Melkon, he moved his family again to a small three room dilapidated shack made of stucco, where he could live rent free in exchange for protecting the premises from vandals.

Michael was recalled to Wilson Foundry in late 1932 for one or two days a week and worked steadily for four months, but was then laid off again for over a year. During this period of inactivity Wilson Foundry provided Michael a sack of flour and potatoes once a week. Victoria learned to make bread and donuts on a broken gas stove. They spent nothing on clothes or entertainment, ate very little, walked everywhere.

One frigid January morning, Victoria answered a knock at the front door and found a heavyset man in overalls standing before her.

"I'm from Edison," he said. "Sorry, got to shut off the meter."

"What for?" Victoria asked.

He looked embarrassed. "Edison let your bill go for three months now. Have to pay me today or I shut off electricity."

"How much we owe?"

"Seven dollars, seventy cents."

"You wait here. Be right back."

Victoria rushed to the bedroom and pulled her little suitcase out of the closet; the money was still there, tied up in the handkerchief, all eight dollars she had saved by not spending the allowance from Cousin Dick. She ran back and hastily thrust the money into his extended hand. "Don't touch electric, please."

He grinned, wrote out a receipt, saying, "I don't like to turn people's electric off, ma'am. I'm glad you could pay."

Victoria nodded. "Iss better to save money for rainy day. Always a time you need it more."

Many times during the winter of 1934 Michael pulled Johnny's small red wagon to the train station and filled it with used coal found along the railroad tracks. One night when the temperature was near zero, the ashes in the potbellied stove were so heavy that the flue fell apart, filling the room with ashes and smoke and eliminating the fire in the heater.

"The stove!" Victoria yelled to her husband. "Get up and fix the stove. We will freeze. Johnny will get sick."

"All right, all right," Michael mumbled. "I can't sleep with you nagging and complaining. I fix it." He got up, gathered together the parts and repaired the flue.

Victoria snuggled under a blanket, holding Johnny close to keep him from the cold. "I never had anyone to look over me, but don't worry, I never let that happen to you."

*   *   *   *

Michael didn't like the idea of having to accept free food from the Welfare Agency and thus refused all offers. He wanted to work and provide for the family by his own deeds, not through the charity of others. He frequented the Welfare office in hopes of landing the work which seemed to elude him in recent months. When the agency learned he had once repaired shoes in the Old Country, the officials gave him work three times a week, as well as precious coal for heat.

The following month, cousin Melkon rushed over with the news that the cramped two-bedroom upstairs attic space at his house was available. Michael agreed to move his family back to Melkon's in the winter of 1935 and share the supply of the coveted coal.

In September of that year the foundry called Michael back to work part time, grinding chunks of iron taken from tubs of molten metal. Often pieces of hot steel would fly into his eyes through the sides of his safety goggles. When he paused to clean his eyes the foreman would ostracize him for laziness; Michael never talked back, realizing in order to feed his family he needed this work.

When the verbal abuse by the foreman became intolerable, Michael threatened to quit. The supervisor, who had taken a liking to Michael after noticing hard, diligent and consistent work, persuaded him to take a week off and report back under a new foreman. He agreed, but knew that the foundry was not for him and that his days there were numbered. He worked three days a week at the factory and the rest of the time was spent repairing shoes at the Welfare office.

*   *   *   *

Early in November, 1935, while walking to work, Michael ran into the leather salesman, Smith, whom he knew moderately well. Smith had told him about a man in Detroit he had just seen who was looking to sell his shoe equipment. Michael said, "Tell me his name. I'm interested in the shoe business."

"How you gonna pay for a business?"

"I have a one-hundred-dollar life insurance policy from years ago. I could collect on that and use it to buy the machinery."

Smith asked, "Where would you put them and how are you going to get them there? They weigh a ton."

"I know a store I can rent, and have a friend with six sons and a truck."

Smith laughed and said, "Okay. I'll put you in touch with this guy if you really want to follow this, but it's probably going to be expensive." The two men shook hands and Michael walked home with energy in his step.

The following week the owner of the equipment company agreed to meet with Michael. Impressed with his determination to buy the machinery despite economic setbacks, the owner agreed to sell the machines and the leather goods for a down payment of forty dollars, with the balance deferred until the business started to make money. Michael convinced his friend with the six sons to move the heavy machinery from Detroit to a small store in Pontiac for six dollars. Once the deal was complete, Michael told Victoria.

"Are you out of your mind? You're going to borrow forty dollars?" She leaned toward him, her face red, the veins in her neck sticking out. "We don't have money for food, and you want to get us deeper in debt? How are you going to pay off the forty dollars?" She shouted at him, arms passionately waving in the air.

Michael's face twisted in anger. "Don't you worry. This is *my* business. I find a way."

"With your way, we be out in the streets."

"You don't know what you're talking about. I am the head of this family. You listen to me!"

Victoria stood up and shoved her chair under the table. "From now on, don't ask me nothing. Go...learn your lesson."

She stalked out from the room and slammed the bedroom door.

Michael borrowed the forty dollars from cousin Melkon and gave the previous owner the agreed upon down payment. Papers were signed which showed that Michael was now the legal owner of a shoe business. The store opened with Victoria, now three months pregnant with the second child, agreeing to mind the store while Michael worked at the foundry. When he finished his day at Wilson, he came home and relieved his wife, who would give him all of the day's orders and he would work late into the evening repairing shoes. For months the business didn't take in more than five cents a day, but gradually customers began to bring in their shoes after hearing good word of mouth. Consequently in March, 1936, business began to improve to a point where Michael was able to quit working at the foundry altogether and devote all of his time to shoe repair.

Victoria no longer worked at the store once Michael started full time. She focused on washing and cleaning straight through her ninth month of pregnancy. Again and again she went up and down two long flights of stairs to wash clothes, frequently having to stop to rest. She would scrub the wooden floors by hand, back aching, ignoring the splinters that caught in her swollen hands. Faint from the suffocating Michigan summer heat, she frequently carried her mattress out to the back porch at night and slept until dawn.

When Victoria started to have labor pains one evening, Michael called Dr. Castell at once. Because Victoria was experiencing intense pain, the doctor wanted to stay close by her, so he slept downstairs at cousin Melkon's house. Louis, who had moved in with them in 1935, usually occupied the second bedroom upstairs but he also slept downstairs for the night in order that Victoria might have privacy.

Near dawn her water broke. Her screams woke Michael, Dr. Castell, and Melkon's wife, Mariam, who eagerly rushed to her side to witness the birth. Dr. Castell assisted her with breathing while instructing Michael and Mariam, who both could hardly contain themselves.

On July 22nd, at nine o'clock in the morning during
the hottest day of the year, a daughter was born to Victoria
and Michael. Michael could not pay the birth expense, so
Dr. Castell again agreed to let him work as his gardener
and handyman for one year until the debt was paid.

Feeling satisfied that mother and daughter were
doing well, Michael left for work later that morning. In the
evening Mariam prepared supper and at the dinner table
Michael turned to Louis, who was Godfather, and asked,
"What shall we name her?"

"How about Virginia? I've always like the name of
that state."

"Virginia is *Vehrsheen* in Armenian. I like that. It is
decided."

Victoria was overwhelmed with the responsibilities of
caring for two small children. Johnny, who was now seven,
did not help with any housework or caring for his new
sister. Nevertheless, she didn't mind the work. It kept
order in her world and the hours of her day varied and
filled. The children were noisy, messy and demanding,
requiring hugs and kisses and games. Needs that were
overwhelming to someone unused to giving such attention.
Eventually, Victoria turned to her housekeeping; the
scrubbing and cleaning gave her comfort, yet the more she
scrubbed the less time she had to pay attention to her
children.

Michael and Victoria had been married seven years,
and Michael was unable to keep his promise of sending his
wife back to New York to visit her cousins, who were
without work and money. Letters could not replace their
absence; that year she saved two dollars from the grocery
money and mailed it to them for Christmas.

About a year later, Michael was busy repairing shoes
in his rented shop when he heard an unusual tapping
sound outside which aroused his curiosity. He stopped his
work and looked out his window where he saw a man
hammering a "For Sale" sign into the lawn of the house
next door. Michael rushed out to him. "If this house is for
sale, I would like to buy it. Please take the sign down."

The man nodded. "All right. I need a deposit of fifty
dollars to seal the bargain."

Michael returned to the cash box in his shop and came back with fifty dollars, which he had been saving since starting the business two years before.

He returned home that evening prepared to face Victoria's wrath.   But he had grown accustomed to her nagging complaints, sudden fits of anger and constant carping. He never enjoyed this, but it didn't sway him from the decision to buy the house. To his surprise, however, Victoria was quite pleased. For the first time there was no complaint over the expense involved...because now they wouldn't have to live with relatives.

Three weeks later Michael and Victoria signed the Home and Loan Company's papers to purchase the $2,200.00 farmhouse with payments of a hundred and fifty dollars a month.

The house stood at the corner of two dirt roads, Prospect and Sanford, in Pontiac. The old farmhouse had a porch across the front and down one side, with a long railing of white spindle-shaped posts that looked like an apron tied around the middle of the house. It had thirteen windows, which meant that Victoria didn't have to sleep on the porch to enjoy the fresh air. Back in the Old Country, houses were made of mud bricks with oiled-paper windows; with dirt floors, no electricity or plumbing, no heating system. This house had none of those inconveniences. A pantry off the kitchen led to a small room set off from the main part of the farmhouse, which Michael would use for his shoe business one year later. The large kitchen had a square table in the center and four aluminum chairs, an ice-box, running water, and a cooking stove not quite as rusty as the one in the previous house. The two oak doors closing the parlor off from the dining room had small framed windows. Old fashioned lace curtains covered the parlor's front windows that spilled shafts of sunlight onto the shiny oak floor.

Victoria's house.

Chapter 5

On a humid September morning in 1941, Virginia clung to her mother's hand as they walked two blocks to Wilson Elementary for her first day of kindergarten.

"*Myreeg*, (mother) please," she sobbed. "I don't want to go to school."

Victoria snapped, "You're afraid because you don't speak English very well."

"Don't leave me, Myreeg."

Victoria gripped Virginia's hand. "The law says you got to go to school. Going to school is a privilege."

When they arrived at the school office, the tall, earnest Finnish principal, Mr. Wargelin, smiled to Virginia amid the girl's protests and said that she would be fine with them.

Victoria pried nervous, desperate little fingers from her hand, mumbled a barely audible goodbye and turned her back on the wailing child.

After Victoria left, Mr. Wargelin consoled the child by smiling. "Welcome to our school, Virginia. I know you're going to enjoy it here. Your teacher's name is Mrs. Cagle. Come along, I'll take you to her room." He waited patiently a few moments for Virginia to stop crying before escorting her to the classroom, knowing it was better that she went willingly rather than him having to carry her. He held the child's hand in his, pointing to various areas of interest within the school which included the gym, the art room and library; all the while she only looked at his heels.

When Mr. Wargelin opened the door to the class-room, Virginia's eyes widened. She saw a heavyset lady with peppery black and white curly hair wearing thick horn rimmed glasses, sitting across the room on a high spindle stool with her back to a piano, reading *The Three Little Pigs* to thirty boys and girls sitting cross-legged on the floor.

Mr. Wargelin cleared his throat. "Excuse the interruption, Mrs. Cagle, but I bring you a new student. I'd like to introduce Virginia Haroutunian, who speaks mostly Armenian and very little English."

Mrs. Cagle smiled and nodded. "How do you say her name, Har...out...un...?"

The class broke out in laughter. Virginia took her hand from the principal and darted behind his left leg, taking firm hold of polyester pants. He reached out a burly hand and gently brought the resistant child from hiding to face the class. He looked to the teacher and repeated the pronunciation. "It's Har-ou-tun-ian." He turned to the class and sternly reproached them for the impoliteness of laughing at strange sounding names.

After Mr. Wargelin left, Mrs. Cagle motioned to Virginia. "Come, come." She walked over and took the newcomer's hand and led the nervous child through the subdued group of children, all of whom were still stunned by the principal's admonishment. "In a few days, with a little practice, I'll be able to pronounce your name." She turned to the other students. "Class, say hello to Virginia." Virginia stood before everyone; Mrs. Cagle was behind, resting her hands on quivering shoulders.

"Hello, Virginia," they mimicked back. A few of the boys made silly gestures toward her funny brown banana curls or pointed to her checkered brown and white dress and black lace-up oxfords; gestures which made several others laugh. Virginia shrank. When Mrs. Cagle pointed to an empty space, she quickly sat. The eyes and ears of the students returned to the teacher's storytelling and Virginia relaxed long enough to begin observing this strange, unusual new place filled with a variety of faces, sounds and images. Of special interest was the playroom, consisting of a yellow slide, ironing board and iron, a big white dollhouse with miniature dishes, pots, pans and furniture and giant rag dolls with red banana curls.

After the storytelling the teacher played the piano and the students sang and clapped to the rhythm of "If you're happy and you know it, clap your hands." Virginia let the first verse pass, but saw that her classmates were having such fun, and felt left out. Noting that the others were so involved, she felt safe from observation and happily joined the chorus.

When the song came to an end, Mrs. Cagle announced that it was play time. Cheers went up from the students, who quickly scattered about the room to be the first at the slide or the dollhouse or to find their favorite games; Virginia was too timid to move toward any of the activities. A few of the girls approached in hopes of persuading her to join them, but she only shook her head and looked down at the floor.

Mrs. Cagle took Virginia by the hand and led her to the large dollhouse, where several girls and even two boys were playing house. She asked one girl, Armida, who Virginia could be in the family and Armida enthusiastically said she could be her sister. Armida went to Virginia and asked which name she wanted to use, saying that she was a Sally, so that name could not be chosen. "Nancy," was the quiet reply. It was thus decided: Sally and Nancy became sisters in the Smith family. Together they pretended to cook, clean, and converse like their parents.

After playtime Mrs. Cagle led the class out for recess, where several other classes were already out. Virginia was disoriented and more than a little intimidated at the observation of much older students. Moreover, seeing swings and jungle gyms, plastic baseball bats and students chasing each other wildly were all new and strange sights. One classmate was being chased by two boys who were reaching out with thin arms to grab handfuls of pigtailed hair. Virginia, with hands thrust deep into her pockets and back hunched against the brick building, watched with fright as the two boys captured the girl and pulled on her braids while taunting her with accusations of bad breath and head lice. Mrs. Cagle ran to separate the quarreling children and then summoned the class back into the building. She walked over to her newest student, gently took her hand, and escorted her in with the others.

"It's time for rest period, Virginia." She instructed the others to get a quilt from one of the closets and lay on the floor; no one was to open their eyes or speak for the next fifteen minutes. Mrs. Cagle handed Virginia a quilt and instructed her to follow the class example. Virginia laid on a spot, obeying the teacher, yet her eyes fluttered open and closed with impatient restlessness.

After rest period Mrs. Cagle asked each of the children to paint a picture. She brought out the paints, brushes, and construction paper and laid them across a long rectangular table. Sitting next to her new friend Armida, Virginia painted a bright yellow sun with a wide smiling face in the upper right hand corner. She used red to draw a little schoolhouse and painted tall green grass all around it. Standing at the front door was a young girl with banana curls wearing a big smile, her arms were around her father while her mother was to the left, smiling with hands at her sides. Armida watched closely, offering her criticisms.

Kindergarten was half day sessions. Victoria arrived early that first day to take Virginia home, waiting outside the classroom door for dismissal.

Mrs. Cagle led the smiling girl to her mother, saying, "Mrs. Har-ou-tun-ian, Virginia did well today." Victoria nodded politely and took Virginia's hand, leading her home.

*   *   *   *

The kindergarten days passed with greater frequency as Virginia began to take greater interest in her classmates and the class activities. She was able to participate with the others and made friends easily. At recess she became confident enough to approach nearly any friend and participate on any of the playground facilities. School for her became a place of acceptance and fun.

Chapter 6

By the time Virginia was in the second grade, America was embroiled in World War II. Michael had tried to enlist in the Army but was rejected because he was over forty and considered too old. He subsequently volunteered to serve as an Air Raid Warden and was accepted for his area in Pontiac. The Air Raid Warden was required to make sure all streets were clear at night of traffic and pedestrians, and that all street and building lights were turned out once the sun set, and in cases of emergency, during the day as well. This was done to prevent any possible air attacks from finding targets. At the Warden's disposal were several messengers to assist in the implementation; this gave Michael a tremendous surge of pride. He was leading men and women instead of following, and was entrusted with an important responsibility. In his mind this was an honorable duty for his country.

Despite this new responsibility, Michael still labored in his shoe shop, which had moved in the narrow room past the pantry in the house. Against one wall he placed a large wooden platform, on top of which stood the large black velvet arm chair where customers would sit and place their feet on the two iron shoe-rests, where he would give his renowned expert, spotless, shoe shine. Because shoes were rationed, people were having old pairs mended and thus business was on the constant increase.

When there were no customers in the shop, Virginia pretended the chair was a "throne." She would sit and slide up the length of the cushion until her feet touched the shoe-rests, and would watch her father go about repairing shoes. When a customer wanted a "ten-cent spit shine" she hopped down and stood nearby to watch the gooey, thick, paste-like polish being applied to the customer's shoes, and then saw them buffed until the narrow rag snapped and crackled. This was her favorite after school activity. She spent nearly all her free time with *Hyreeg* (father), who never seemed to mind. Michael grew to enjoy her company; with Virginia he was always patient, cheerful and supportive. He took great pride in her achievements, as she consistently brought home good grades and high praise from her teachers. For each A on her report card he gave one dollar. They would often take long walks together after dinner; where they would hold hands and sing, "A-Rig-a-Jig-Jig," skipping to the refrain. Whenever Myreeg accompanied them, she never skipped.

While Virginia was flamboyant and never lacking energy, Victoria's house was her world. She had no close friends, seldom visited neighbors, refused to join any clubs or guilds, not even any Armenian groups. She had her family, but whenever Michael's relatives came to visit and play cards, Victoria would always remain in the background, watching passively.

By the time Virginia was seven, she realized that her mother only showed affection when someone was sick. If Virginia had a fever or stomach ailment, Myreeg would stroke the top of her head, tell Armenian folk tales, make delicious hot chicken broth with lemon juice, toast, and offer healing medicines. At times Virginia looked forward to being sick as it meant hearing such fables as *Rooster Brother*, a tale Victoria's mother had passed down to her about an intelligent rooster who stole the clothes of three unsuspecting bandits sitting in a bath house.

When Virginia was eight her mother thought her grown enough to travel on the bus with her to Pontiac for shopping excursions. She would often try to convince Myreeg to buy her a new Easter Sunday dress or patent leather sandals; each time Victoria would snap at the young girl, "There's no money for fancy clothes. You have plenty dresses. I only had one dress that I wore for years."

Virginia disliked hearing her mother's stories of not having clothes or shoes and would cover her ears whenever talk shifted to that subject. "What does this have to do with me?" she thought. "All I want is a new dress. Armida and Dolly will be showing off their new dresses at school and I'll be wearing my old ones. Myreeg is stingy. She won't spend a penny for anything!"

Spirits were always brightened, however, when the shopping trip concluded at Kresge's. A snack bar sold twenty-five cent hot dogs that were always a special treat after the long walking through the department stores, through Waites and Sears, across the street to Federal's, and down two blocks to Fields. Victoria allowed Virginia one hot dog, which she always devoured hungrily and promptly begged for another. With a stern frown Victoria always refused.

"Please, Myreeg, I'm starving," was always the argument.

"No! One is enough! *Haireekeh*! (Enough said)."

Virginia, in angry frustration, would stalk off to a small stage nearby to witness a man playing songs from the "Hit Parade" on a black baby grand piano. Standing by the stage in hypnotic fascination, she was intrigued by the sound and the way his fingers seemed to effortlessly skip over the polished keys. She would lapse into enchanted bliss every time the man played, especially whenever he performed Chopin. Harsh reality always returned when Victoria would grab her hand and drag her from the store.

In fourth grade, Virginia took to music class and especially her teacher, Mrs. Lord, a woman who played the piano impeccably. While teaching she was never angry or cross, but instead encouraging even the most untalented students. She favored Virginia because she demonstrated an energetic willingness to learn the piano and a capacity to maintain rhythms. Virginia was always chosen to play the block in rhythm band, a disagreeable choice because its sound was so obvious that it drew unwanted attention. Yet it was the most important part of the band, as it kept the tempo consistent for the other instruments. Dismissal for her was ten minutes early every day so that she might cross the street and buy Mrs. Lord a hamburger and coffee for lunch. This act of responsibility always left the feeling of great importance.

Whenever students were asked for their favorite songs, Virginia was the first to answer by requesting "Celito Lindo," because singing the Ay, ay, ay, ays and swaying to

the music were enormous fun; her second favorite was
Funnicali, Funnicala," because Mrs. Lord would play the
chorus faster and faster after each verse.

The week before Christmas students caroled in the
hall every day before school began. The second floor had a
railing which circled the balcony; a giant Christmas tree
extended from the first floor through the opening to the
second floor. The multi-colored blinking lights and paper
mache student art decorations pooled together with gold
and silver tinsel made for a spectacular sight. Mrs. Lord
would play the piano, which was rolled out from the music
room, and all the students would sit on the first floor and
sing. The traditional conclusion to this festivity came when
the buxomly first grade teacher, Mrs. Kohn, sang "Silent
Night" in a lovely vibrato. Virginia was always in a trance.

At the dinner table one night she begged Michael to
buy a piano for her ninth birthday. "Music is inside me. I
want to play the piano."

Michael put down his fork and stared for a moment
before answering, "I would love to hear music in our home,
Vehrsheen. But there's a war on, and pianos are expensive
and hard to come by." He was stern, yet reddened eyes
revealed a hint of genuine regret.

Six months later she returned from school one day
to find an upright piano and matching bench placed
against the dining room wall. Her screams of joy
resounded through the entire house, bringing Michael in
from his shop and Victoria from the kitchen. "Oh thank
you, Hyreeg, it's beautiful!" she cried. She hugged and
kissed him, tears running down her cheeks.

"Vehrsheen," he said, "this is your birthday present
from Myreeg and me."

"Oh thank you, Myreeg!" she cried, arms still
around her father.

"That piano cost too much," Victoria said glumly.
"And lessons not cheap." Dark eyes stared at Virginia. "We
need the money for new stove."

Myreeg's words quelled the joyful enthusiasm and
Virginia swallowed a harsh retort and instead said, "I
promise I'll practice every single day." Sitting on the
bench, she ran her fingers over the piano's smooth

mahogany wood, gingerly pressing the keys and being rewarded with magical sounds.

Knowing Virginia was impatient to master the piano and Victoria was unhappy with the expense, Michael quickly arranged for lessons at an obscure music studio that was not noted for its extravagance, located three blocks upstreet at the end of an alley. The following day after school, Michael met Virginia and escorted her to the first lesson.

He introduced his daughter to Miss Roth, a slim, curly-haired lady with the longest fingers Virginia had ever seen. Miss Roth smiled warmly and said, "I know you will study hard and be one of my best pupils." She turned to Michael as if to anticipate any concern. "Private music students always do well in school, too." Michael nodded politely and left the two to begin the lesson.

The lessons with Miss Roth began well. Virginia noted visible progress from consistent, diligent and conscientious work and Miss Roth was never at a loss for lavish praise. Music became an outlet for discovering self-confidence and worth. Virginia tended to gravitate toward teachers like Miss Roth, who recognized contributions and praised them. Another such teacher was Mrs. Heimke, the energetic, firm but fair gym teacher who constantly encouraged her students to compete while observing high standards of good sportsmanship. For softball games she allowed students to vote for a team captain. Virginia was frequently chosen, a source of great happiness as it allowed her to pick girlfriends for the team. After choosing teams, the captains would take a baseball bat, each placing one hand at the neck and alternate hands up to the top; the captain whose hand rested on the top always got to bat first. When Virginia was not a captain she took pride in being Mrs. Heimke's assistant, passing out the equipment, taking roll, and all other necessary tasks.

Gradually, however, music became the central focus of her life. The piano lessons continued to a point where she could play "Rachmaninoff's Prelude in C Sharp Minor," which led Miss Roth to invite her to play in the upcoming spring recital.

"You think I'm good enough to play for an audience?" she asked with cautious enthusiasm.

"Yes, indeedee," Miss Roth replied with a wide smile. "The piano will be placed in the middle of the studio, with folding chairs around it. I have four students whom I've chosen to play and you will be the last. Be sure to invite your parents."

Virginia was so excited that she ran all the way home and rushed into the kitchen. "Myreeg! Guess what? I'm going to be in a recital! All the parents will be there. You and Hyreeg can come to hear me play!"

"Your father can't come. He works. Can't leave shop alone. I don't know if I come," she said impatiently. "Have a lot of housework. I'm only one who does work here, you never help with anything. I don't promise to be there."

On the day of the recital, Virginia's hopes were high. She walked directly to the studio after school, music in hand, and went to the front row. People were already starting to gather but Myreeg was not among them. Virginia watched the entrance closely until the recital began, at which time she shifted attention to a last minute review of the music, remembering the chords, accidentals, fingerings, dynamics and tempo, all of which had taken months to perfect. The three previous students played well and finally her turn had come. Miss Roth announced, "Virginia Haroutunian will now perform 'Rachmaninoff's Prelude to C Sharp Minor.'"

Virginia looked into the audience as she walked toward the piano, hoping that Myreeg had decided to come. She felt her face grow warm and hands tremble, noting Myreeg's absence.

Miss Roth spoke again, "Virginia? Are you ready?"

The young girl brushed the tears off her cheeks with the back of her hand, nodded and took in a deep breath. She played perfectly, but without feeling.

*   *   *   *

Virginia used music as an escape from the sound of her mother's harsh criticisms and frequent temper; as time continued she delighted in doing whatever her music demanded while reveling in not doing what her mother expected.

Victoria hollered, "Whenever I ask you to help me, you play the piano. Why can't you be like other girls your age? They do what they are told right away without talking back."

"I have to practice," Virginia hollered back. "Hyreeg says education is more important than housework. How can I learn if I don't practice?"

"*Haireekeh*! Enough said. It's your father's fault anyway that you never listen to me. He spoil you."

Myreeg's scolding was always dodged by running to Hyreeg's shop. Curled up in the soft velvet throne she drifted into a make-believe world of music, picturing herself as the pianist at Carnegie Hall playing "Mozart's Concerto in A Major." Behind was the New York Philharmonic Orchestra, conducted by Arturo Toscanini, but all eyes were transfixed on her. When the final cadence was played the audience would rise to a standing ovation and an usher approached with a dozen long-stemmed red roses; numerous other roses were enthusiastically thrown onto the stage by adoring fans. Myreeg was never in the audience.

Victoria's angry voice would always cut short these daydreams.

"Vehrsheen! Vehrsheen! Come here!"

Virginia jumped down and ran through the pantry into the kitchen, yelling, "*Inch goo zess?* What do you want?"

Her mother stood at the stove, frying perch. "What do I want? What do you think? I can't do all this work alone. Stop standing around and help me."

Virginia gritted her teeth. "Myreeg, I'm going outside to play. My friends are waiting for me."

"No you're not! Tell your friends to go home. You got work to do here. When I was your age, I stayed in the house all day."

Virginia ran out the door into the fresh air, muttering, "I hate her."

Chapter 7

Though the Armenian church was a long distance
from their house, Victoria always insisted that the family
attend Easter services. For Virginia it was an exciting day
because it gave the opportunity to ask for a new dress. It
was the only time that Myreeg said no to her and reversed
that decision.

Virginia had never understood the liturgy, spoken in
classical Armenian, and thus gave up trying after a few
years finding that the well-dressed congregation was a
more interesting subject to observe. It was fun to look
about the congregation to find the best-dressed lady with
the fanciest hat. Pastel straw bonnets covered with colorful
flowers, veiling, ribbons and pins dotted the nave of the
church like a colorful bouquet. Victoria wore a mauve
linen sheath dress, a black and white straw hat with a
band of black sequins above the trim, tilted on one side of
her head. Virginia wore a taffeta light pink dress that had
a ballerina skirt and a white straw hat with a navy blue
satin ribbon that tied under her chin.

The organ music sounded in the minor key with its
slow march-like rhythm. Virginia paid close attention to
the careful, subtle participation of the organist, who played
the pedalpoint while the choir sang the melody of *Der
Vorghmia*, a response sung by the deacons and choir.
Myreeg's reaction was always the same; unmoved, staring
straight ahead.

After church the relatives gathered at a nearby
cousin's home for holiday celebration. The festivities
always started with an Easter egg game, which brought
participation from the entire Haroutunian clan. A basket of
hard-boiled reddish brown eggs boiled with onion skins

was passed to each family member. The object was to hit an opponent's egg with theirs and vice versa. After this, whoever's egg shell remained uncracked was declared the winner. Michael usually let Virginia win when they were opponents, but she nearly always lost later when an eager cousin deliberately hit her egg so that it would break.

After the egg game the family bowed their heads and said The Lord's Prayer in Armenian before sitting to a large meal of chicken, pilaf and salad, which had been carefully prepared by the hostess. To show gratitude each family presented her with a small gift, usually a bottle of wine or a box of Saunders chocolates or an Easter plant of lilies. All would eat until the food and wine were gone and then sit back and play *Scambill,* a card game where one gave their teammate facial signals to tell their hand. The object was for the other team not to see the signals and to get the most points by utilizing the trump cards. The ace was worth four points, kings 3, queens 2, jacks 1, and all other cards under the jack were pointless except for the trump cards.

The Armenian culture was vibrant and alive in the Haroutunian household. Hyreeg would sing the ballads that depicted Armenian history, special songs that had been handed down over the centuries from fathers to sons which detailed battles, the laments of soldiers, and the spirit of patriotism. Michael, Victoria and other community members were instrumental in starting an Armenian school which held classes on Saturdays in an Armenian coffee house. The school was designed to teach children to read and write Armenian as well as teach them of their heritage. Virginia resisted attending at first, complaining that Armenian education was not important—the American school gave her all the education she needed.

"You can never have too much learning, Vehrsheen," Myreeg said. "Look at me, I wanted to go to school more than anything, I never got to learn what you take for granted. No one can take education away from you."

Virginia reluctantly attended the school, though it was more out of interest in the tobacco infested coffee shop full of men drinking strong black coffee in demitasse and playing backgammon while arguing politics. Women were not allowed, but she passed through anyway to the basement where the classes were held.

Virginia hated to admit it, but the melodic sounds of the Armenian language, the beauty of the music, poetry and dances became more intriguing with each successive lesson. She learned a nursery rhyme which quickly became a favorite:

> *Vehrsheen nyem yes, var ar-rev-ee bess.*
> *Garmir tou-shig-ner ooh neem. Tune inch ga guard zess?*

> My name is Vehrsheen. I'm like the setting sun.
> My cheeks are red. What do you think about that?

                    *   *   *   *

Every April 24th Victoria and Michael took Johnny and Virginia to church for Martyr's Day, commemorating the 1915 Armenian Genocide. When Virginia was nine in 1945 they observed the 30th Anniversary. The children were too young to understand the historical complexities, yet both sensed it was a solemn occasion and were always well behaved. Men wore black arm bands, women small black ribbons pinned to their collars; the congregation lit candles, murmured prayers and wept. Virginia watched her parents closely: Hyreeg's eyes were closed, head was bowed, his hands over forehead. Myreeg sat stiffly staring straight ahead.

As Michael and his family left the Church, the ushers gave them *Madagh*, boiled lamb sandwiches. *Madagh* was a thank offering practiced in ancient times where the gathering would share in eating the sacrificial lamb, one of the old pagan customs that had survived to the day.

While driving home, Hyreeg turned to his children and said, "Never forget the words of our Armenian president, Avedis Aharonian:

'If this much blood can be forgiven by our children, let the whole world rightfully insult us all.'"

*   *   *   *

In mid-December, Victoria, Johnny, and Virginia walked to a nearby lot to buy a Christmas tree. Victoria and Johnny argued over the size, shape and price of the pine trees. At fifteen, Johnny was taller than his mother and hard to handle.

"Here, Myreeg, look at this one!" He pointed to the tallest, most expensive one on the lot. "Buy this beauty!"

"Are you crazy? That tree much too big for our room. Too expensive!"

"Aw...you're such a cheapskate! You never get anything good. Always the smallest, the ugliest, the cheapest. Why are you afraid to spend a little money?"

"Shut up! You don't know what it's like to be poor. We have to save our money for rainy days." Walking over to a scrawny little tree marked down to half-price, she announced, "We take this one."

The tree had no appeal. Johnny dragged it down the street, grumbling. Virginia walked behind, offering no opinion.

At home, they continued to argue over where to put the tree and what decorations to use. Victoria would always command Johnny.

"You so stupid, Johnny. Lights go on first. Don't you know that? Then the popcorn strings and glass balls last. I'm not born in this country and even I know these things. Be careful now or you break them."

Virginia sat nearby stringing popcorn, watching them closely.

Pow! The sound of glass breaking reverberated through the room.

"You clumsy ox! Look at what you've done!" Victoria yelled, pointing to the box of glass balls that had been stepped on. "You never do anything right! My favorite ball I got from the World's Fair was in that box. Gone." She reached out and whacked him on the arm.

Johnny danced away, laughing. "So what, so what! It was an accident. Who cares! It's just a dumb old ball."

"Wait till I get my hands on you." Victoria grabbed a broom and gave chase around the oak dining room table, swinging it like a club. Johnny managed to stay out of reach, continuing to taunt, which only increased Myreeg's anger. Eventually, she ran from the room toward the shoe shop.

Virginia, knowing that Myreeg had gone to get Hyreeg into the argument, rushed into the dining room and hid under the large oak table. Johnny was in for it now.

Broom still in hand, Victoria marched into the shoe shop yelling, "Michael, for the love of God, talk some sense into your son. He don't listen to me. He just make big mess in the parlor."

Michael glowered at Myreeg, turned to his customer and said, "Excuse me, I'll be right back."

Sure enough, Hyreeg marched into the living room with Myreeg close behind and glanced at the half-decorated tree and the smashed balls on the floor. Johnny stood by the door, eyes wary, ready to bolt.

"Johnny smashed the whole box of balls. He pay no attention to me."

"It was an accident," he hollered back. "I tried to help her decorate, but she's always yelling at me so I can't think."

Hyreeg stared from Victoria to Johnny, then walked over to the tree, picked it up decorations and all, and slammed it to the floor hollering, "I've had enough of this. How can I run a business with you interrupting me with these stupid arguments? *Der Vorghmia Adzvadz!* Lord have mercy!"

He turned toward Johnny. "You listen to your mother or you get in trouble." He shook his finger in Johnny's face. "But you listen to me or I make you sorry. You hear?" Johnny nodded. Michael glared at Victoria. "Don't you dare bother me when I am working. You hear? Settle nonsense like this yourself." He stalked out of the room and back to the customer.

Complete silence reigned until Michael was out of earshot, then Johnny laughed. "That didn't get you anywhere, Myreeg. Pa just got mad at you." He grabbed his coat and ran outside.

From under the table Virginia watched Myreeg slump into a chair, white-faced and stunned, staring at the pile of broken ornaments and the tree lying on its side.

"Why did Michael get so upset?" asking aloud to herself. "I need him to discipline Johnny. That's a father's job. It's his fault Johnny no listen to me. Makes it hard for me." Looking around. "Vehrsheen? Where did you go?"

"I'm over here," was her faint reply.

Myreeg got up, still clutching the broom, and began sweeping up the mess. Virginia stayed crouched under the table, still trembling.

*   *   *   *

Virginia liked to follow Hyreeg down to the basement when he tended to the furnace and stoked the fire. She would wait for him to pull open the heavy iron door and shovel in the coal, then watched the red and yellow flames dance and engulf them.

"Don't stand so close," he cautioned, tugging her from the open door. "The flames could leap out at you."

While he finished shoveling, Virginia snooped among the piles of junk on the floor and shelves. An old dusty suitcase caught her eye, a peculiar size and shape she'd never seen before. "What's in this?" she asked.

Michael glanced at the suitcase and said, "I don't know. Ask your mother."

Virginia grabbed the handle and ran upstairs, calling out, "Look, Myreeg, look what I found."

Her mother stood at the sink, peeling potatoes.

"Did you hear me, Myreeg? Where did this old suitcase come from? Is it yours?"

Victoria gave the suitcase a surprised look. "Where did you find that?"

"In the basement with the other junk."

"What were you doing down there? I ask you to set the table an hour ago."

"But, Myreeg," Virginia protested, "what's in this old suitcase?"

Victoria turned from the sink and finally looked. "Put that away, Vehrsheen. It's not yours. Take it back where it belongs and set the table."

"It looks like a child's suitcase."

"Talking to you is just like talking to the four walls. I ask you to do something and you ignore me."

Grumbling, "Remember the time you ran out of milk? Who went to the store? Me. Last week when we had company, who helped you set the table? Me. You never appreciate what I do."

She laid the suitcase on the floor in the pantry and got the dishes out of the cupboard. When finished setting the table, she asked once again, "Will you tell me about this suitcase? Where did you get it?"

"Put that back! Stop asking questions."

"Why don't you tell me?"

Victoria turned and mumbled through the thin line of her mouth, "For the last time, that dirty suitcase is covered with dust. You're going to get filthy. Put it back!"

Virginia grabbed the handle and headed for the basement door. "Why won't she answer my questions, explain things, instead of arguing and hollering? Teachers don't criticize my every move. Why does Myreeg? The Sunday school teachers smile and praise me. Myreeg doesn't. My friends' mothers don't yell at them. Why is Myreeg always angry?"

She put the strange suitcase back on the shelf.

Chapter 8

In the late forties Virginia began attending regular Sunday worship at a local Methodist church. Because the Armenian church was too far for regular commuting, Victoria encouraged Johnny and Virginia to attend with the Methodists. "Methodists are good people," she told her children. "They help me long time ago, care for me eight years, feed me and other Armenian kids." Her tone became softer and more pronounced when speaking of the missionaries, one of the rare times it seemed to be without anger. Instead, it suggested a complexity of emotions; sadness, fear, happiness, and even a glimpse of sentimentality all at once. Her entire demeanor was, for only a moment, serene and completely at ease; sitting on a kitchen stool, she leaned forward toward her attentive listeners with hands folded in her lap.

Virginia asked, "Tell me more about the missionaries. What were they like?"

Victoria shook her head, "Not now, Vehrsheen."

*   *   *   *

While having had considerable exposure to American kids in elementary school, Virginia never had friendships outside of the classroom and thus American customs were still foreign. The assumption was made that the rituals Myreeg and Hyreeg practiced daily were for the most part normal American activities. It was not until junior high, however, that she began visiting classmates after school and noticed contrasting routines. For example, her method of bathing by sitting on a wooden stool and filling a brass ladle with water from a pail at her feet, dumping it over

herself, was not an American tradition but in fact an old
Armenian method.   Another difference was the independence that the American children seemed to have from their
parents.   Jessica and others were often allowed to go out
on Friday nights to movies and basketball games, whereas
Myreeg and Hyreeg strictly forbade Virginia from going
anywhere without their supervision. Whenever they social-
ized, she was always brought with them. The influence of
American girls soon became obvious. Each time Virginia
returned home from a visit with Jessica, she would say to
Myreeg, "Jessica's folks said she can go to the basketball
game Friday night. Can I go, too?"

Victoria would grumble, "You don't have to do everything your friends do. American parents give their children
too much freedom. Armenian way is better."

Virginia protested, "But we live in America. I want to
be like my American friends. Sometimes they get to make
their own decisions. I never do."

"We tell you what to do because we know what's best
for you. We know what kind of kids you should play with,
you don't. If you go with bad apple, you turn bad. We have
life experience. We know best. Haireekeh! Enough said."

Virginia knew she would never convince Myreeg to
think otherwise. Both parents would persist in the ways of
the Old Country with regard to raising children, which left
her with a growing sense of isolation and depression.
There was an intense longing to be an American—to think
and act like one, to shed all the foreign Armenian values
and customs that molded and restricted her.   At school
girls openly flirted with boys by passing notes back and
forth during class.   She wanted to know what the notes
contained. Were they arranging dates? Describing secret
feelings? She had once practiced writing a note to Steven,
a handsome boy in Science class, but tore it into pieces
and flushed them down the toilet after a fit of timidity,
deciding it was best to conceal her admiration and protect
her own feelings. There was envy with the other girls' ease
in flirting, and yet another part disapproved, for Myreeg
had often said that such behavior was not only improper,
but immoral. Love was to be reserved only for marriage,
and not before. Still, that knowledge could not quell the

desire for a boy's attention; to be noticed was all she wanted.

*   *   *   *

In 1948 the war had been over for two years and the economy was improving steadily. Plenty of jobs were available in the automotive industry at Pontiac Motors and at Fischer Body, both located in the city of Pontiac. Johnny had graduated from high school and wanted to add a shoe retail department to Michael's existing shoe repair shop. The two debated the possible addition for several weeks, Michael being skeptical due to his lack of retail knowledge. However, he knew that if the addition was not made, Johnny would have no place with him and likely be cornered into working at a factory. So, in the spring of 1949, a new addition to the shoe shop was added and the company name changed from "Mike's Shoe Repair" to "Haroutunian & Son." The business was slow in starting and Johnny quickly grew impatient from the paltry financial results. Disregarding his father's suggestion that progress would show after time and experience, Johnny quit after six months to join the Army, being assigned to Fort Knox, Kentucky.

Michael was devastated by the sudden departure. His long standing dream had been a hope that Johnny might go to college and carry the family name with honor out into the business world. Johnny, however, had never shown any interest in books or education and lacked the motivation. The high aspirations Michael held for Johnny to perhaps become a lawyer or doctor, quickly dissolved with his leaving. Michael's hardest lesson to acknowledge was that Johnny did not share in his pursuits, his ideas, his dreams.

Since retail was such an unfamiliarity to Michael, it became a troubled venture, having to enlist Virginia's assistance so that he could focus on the shoe repair work. She would attend the Statler shoe conventions in Detroit to purchase the most competitive inventory, and after school assist with the accounting since Michael understood little the practices of English bookkeeping.

*   *   *   *

Two cliques were readily observed upon Virginia's entrance into high school. The Westsiders came from the wealthier families, wore expensive clothes, dated and belonged to fraternities and sororities. Virginia belonged to the Southsiders—the middle class who couldn't afford expensive clothing, didn't usually date, had no social clubs, and had parent-chaperoned parties in their homes. Victoria would let Virginia go to these events only with the understanding that Michael would drop her off and pick her up.

Virginia's best friend in high school was Jessica Bell, also a Southsider. She was thin, very pretty and popular, outgoing and friendly, always saying the right things. Virginia by contrast was plump, inhibited and withdrawn. Jessica's parents were teachers; Victoria and Michael had little education. Jessica had a steady boyfriend; Virginia was forbidden to date. Virginia constantly compared herself to Jessica, and by her standards never measured up. Frustration was channeled into three routine activities: spending hours at the piano, helping Hyreeg in the store, and eating. She ate constantly—Armenian bread; french fries and hamburgers; havla and chocolates, thus gaining twenty-five pounds in a year.

*   *   *   *

In 1951 Victoria and Michael finally had the means to visit cousins Dick and Harry, who now lived comfortably in Connecticut and worked together at an iron factory in Hartford. Cousin Dick's wife Zevart had separated from him, keeping Gerald with her and remaining in Watervliet. But Dick was in good spirits and animated as ever. Harry Jr., who was now in his thirties, had joined the Merchant Marines. The daughter, Helen, was the sole female presence in their household. She did not work, instead remained home to look after the house.

In early spring they left for the week's vacation. For the long drive, Michael bought a beautiful maroon Chrysler New Yorker, covered with shiny chrome grillwork and trim.

While out East, Michael took the two women to an abandoned farm to teach Victoria how to drive. She got in the driver's seat beside Michael, while Virginia sat in the back to watch.

"Step one," Michael instructed. "Turn the key to the right to start the car."

Victoria tried it, and jumped when the engine started.

"Step two. See the pedal on the left? Push it all the way in with your left foot." Her foot pushed in the clutch. "Now this handle here is the gear shift. Right now it's in neutral. That means the car won't move forward or backward. When you move the handle down here...it's in first gear. The pedal on the right is the accelerator. That makes the car move forward. Slowly push it down with your right foot while slowly releasing the clutch and the car will move. Now try it."

Virginia saw Victoria give Michael a nervous look. "Push in with my foot? Like this? Move gear down like this?"

The car gave a jolt forward with a sickening screech.

"Damn it! You didn't have the pedal all the way down to the floor!"

Victoria winced. "I had my foot on the pedal. It no work."

"It works if you do it right. Try it again. Same thing."

Victoria took a deep breath and tried again. Once more the car jumped forward like a rabbit, screeching until it stalled.

"Jesus, you gonna strip the gears," Michael yelled. "You don't listen. Push the clutch down, all the way down. Do it again."

"No!" Victoria cried. "I don't learn nothing from you. You have no patience, always yell at me." She threw her hands up, got out of the car and slammed the door. "I quit!"

Michael sat there, stunned.

"Teach me, Hyreeg," cried Virginia. "I want to learn to drive."

"Okay. You move up front in driver's seat. Victoria, you get in the back."

Virginia eagerly moved up. Victoria got in the back seat with arms folded across her chest.

Michael gave the same instructions, and the car jumped and gears screeched same as before.

"What am I doing wrong, Hyreeg?   What's the matter?"

"Push clutch down to floor and let out slowly as you push accelerator down with right foot."

Virginia tried again and again, each time it got a little smoother.

"Don't be afraid, Vehrsheen. You're doing okay. You listen to directions good."

Victoria mumbled from the back seat, "Why don't you holler at her? You yell so much and mix up my mind."

Michael laughed.   "Because you can't learn anything. Don't put blame on me. You give up too fast."

*   *   *   *

On Virginia's sixteenth birthday in 1952, she passed the driver's test, a moment as thrilling as the day she received her beloved piano. She had two special talents now—playing the piano and driving the car.

Michael allowed her to drive the Chrysler to school when she got her license, paying no heed to Victoria's vehement objections. Virginia soon realized that girls became her "friend" whenever they wanted a ride, but ignored her while in school.

Victoria said, "I told you, don't give nobody ride. Don't trust people. Your brother gave kids ride, had an accident, and none of his friends show up in court as witness to help. Your father end up paying for all the damages. You never listen to me. You think I don't know nothing."

Not wanting to believe Myreeg was right, Virginia nevertheless stopped giving rides. Consequently the girls stopped talking to her altogether.

Virginia graduated in 1954. Fat and frumpy, she wasn't invited to the senior prom. Several times she had picked up the telephone to call Steven or David to casually ask if they had a date for the prom, but would always hang up after the second ring, too afraid to play the scenario out.

On prom night she stayed in her room all evening, alone and desolate, tormented by visions of girlfriends in their fancy gowns and corsages, dancing in a boy's arms. "Why can't I be thin and pretty like Jessica? Why can't I have a boyfriend?" She threw herself on the bed and sobbed. "I hate me."

The overeating increased. Food and music became her life and yet food was the enemy. Every day she would stand in front of the mirror and vow to diet. "Tomorrow, starting tomorrow I will cut off all sweets and snacks. By the end of the summer I'll be thin and popular. College will be different. I'll have any boy I want."

Chapter 9

Disappointed that Johnny had no interest in going to college, Michael placed his hopes in Virginia, who in 1954 was a senior in high school. The year before graduation he and Victoria discussed the possibility of college.

"Where we get the money?" Victoria asked. "Girls always quit and get married. It's a waste of money, we could use it to expand the business."

Michael shook his head. "No, no. We live on bread and water if we have to. Vehrsheen iss smart girl, look what she did with the music. She can sight-read, play concerto duos with her teacher, and give piano lessons. That take talent, brains and hard work."

"She never help me with the housework. Girls her age should know how to cook, clean house for marriage. Vehrsheen can't do anything."

"Because you don't teach her," Michael said irritably. "I hear you in the kitchen. She asks you questions, but you don't answer. When she marries she learn to cook just like you did." He slapped the table. "It's final. Vehrsheen goes to college. Whichever one she wants."

Virginia was overjoyed at Hyreeg's support and yet dubious of being accepted to the University of Michigan, her first choice. The competition would be stiff so she sent her applications to the University and its School of Music in October of the year prior to her hoped matriculation. One of the requirements for acceptance to the School of Music was a successful audition in front of the music faculty in the autumn. Much of the senior year was spent practicing "The Mozart Concerto in A Major" for the audition; meticulous work eventually yielded near mastery.

A month before graduation, Virginia walked out to the mailbox one afternoon and found a letter from the University. She tore the envelope, reading its contents while running into the house yelling, "Myreeg! Myreeg! I've been accepted. They let me in. Here, read the letter."

"That's nice." She didn't smile or say anything more, instead turned back to dinner preparations.

"How come you're never excited when something good happens to me? Don't you want my life to be happy?" A pause. "Well...don't you?"

Victoria's hands kept busy peeling the potatoes.

"Are you jealous?" she persisted. "Do you wish it was you going off to college?"

Victoria continued peeling. "Yes. I wish it was me."

*   *   *   *

Upon acceptance to the University of Michigan, Virginia continued with greater determination the preparations for her audition. An education at University of Michigan would be regarded with great respect, but Virginia's sights were set specifically on the School of Music, as music had become her life's ambition. The tedious daily rehearsals would last three hours after school. The constant practice showed promise, yet still she worried, making ready for any possible pitfalls, whether it was lost concentration, missed fingerings or misinterpreted dynamics, ensuring that there was a solution for any mistake.

After graduation and with arrival of summer, the daily practice schedule increased to five hours. While her peers were out working or sitting on the beach, Virginia was at the piano every day until her departure, which came on a beautiful early September morning. The Chrysler was packed to capacity with clothes, books, suitcases and other necessities of a young college student. Michael and Victoria drove the fifty miles to Ann Arbor to assist with Virginia's move, arriving in front of Mosher-Jordan Dormitory and observing several girls already huddled at the front entrance. Fair-haired girls, fair-skinned, tall, thin, stylishly dressed and waving long cigarette holders, they laughed together while crowding inside. Virginia's elation quickly gave way to depression; she was olive-skinned, dark-haired, short and pudgy. Her clothes were ordinary. Though a bona fide student at the University of Michigan, there was the feeling that she was out of place. She looked to Myreeg and Hyreeg and thought, "I can't get out of this now. The tuition is paid, and they are counting on me to do well."

The three of them made several trips between car and dorm, carrying all the stashed belongings that Virginia had compiled over her eighteen years. She noted with interest that the other parents were calm and well dressed, speaking proper English. Victoria, by contrast, wore a simple cotton housedress; Michael wore polyester slacks and a white cotton shirt. While standing in line for the elevator both showed impatience by raising their voices to nearly a shout, speaking Armenian excitedly, drawing curious glances from other parents waiting. Virginia, attempting to hide a growing embarrassment by rubbing her forehead, turned to Myreeg and Hyreeg and told them there was no hurry.

When all was unpacked, the three waited to ride the elevator back down to the lobby. A small crowd of other girls stood in front of them. Michael and Victoria each took one of Virginia's hands, preparing to say goodbye. "Be sure to call us every week, Vehrsheen." Michael hugged and kissed her. Victoria added, "Don't waste your money on long-distance calls." She reached into her worn shopping bag and handed Virginia a yellow box of Sunkist prunes. "Eat these every day, Vehrsheen, to keep your bowels emptied." Virginia's face flushed as she dropped the box into her bag, looking around for any witnesses. How could Myreeg pull out such an embarrassing gift? The thought of anyone seeing the box mortified her, yet she did not want to offend the genuine sincerity of Myreeg so she uttered a quick thank you and promised to stay healthy.

They rode the elevator down to the lobby in silence. The inevitable moment of parent-child separation was upon them; the brief delays of buying last minute supplies and forgotten necessities were now finished; there was nothing left for Myreeg and Hyreeg to do, which meant it was time for them to return home. As they walked to the car, Michael made certain Virginia had everything she needed;

each time she nodded, assuring both that all would be well. They embraced one final time for good measure and Virginia helped them into the car. She watched them drive off slowly, smiling at their shouted Armenian phrases of good luck.

She returned to her room to begin settling, hoping to hide the apprehension of her future as effectively as she had hidden the box of prunes. Her roommate, the red-haired Valerie, a girlfriend from high school, was not due to arrive until later that evening.

The following day Orientation Week began. The Dean of Women, a tall, stern lady dressed in tailored clothes, oxford shoes and bobbed hair, welcomed the freshman women.

"You can manage your university life like you care for an automobile," she advised. "You're the driver. Some of you won't even get your car started. Others will fail to make the necessary repairs and your car will stall along the way. The drivers who establish good maintenance habits with regular tune-ups will make it to the finish line. It's entirely up to you."

Both Virginia's parents had said essentially the same thing. "You have a golden opportunity here, Vehrsheen. Don't waste it. Your education is the one thing no one can take from you."

The Dean's pep talk made great sense, and so she relaxed, believing that "good maintenance" practices in high school could be easily applied to college.

The music audition before the jury of four music professors was scheduled for later that week. To calm the growing anxiety, Virginia thought of the sage advice of an old piano teacher, Mr. Morgan, who once told her that, "If you get nervous before beginning to play, just fold your hands together at your waist, look directly at your audience and say to yourself, 'I can do it, you bastards;' then calmly announce your selection."

The audition was held in a carpeted studio with a black concert baby grand piano at the far end of the room. Virginia had never played on a baby grand before, and it was worrisome because her touch was strong and pounding the keys too hard might cause the deep rich tones of the piano to erupt into unpleasant cacophony.

The four professors sat directly in front of the piano and Virginia stood facing them with hands calmly clasped together over her waist. She recalled old Mr. Morgan's advice, turned to the jury and announced her selection.

She began to play and within seconds forgot about all else, drifting into a private world of music without realizing that she was expressing emotions freely. There was no stop in the middle nor was there a loss of concentration, nor any misplayed notes. Yet at the conclusion there was still a feeling of uncertainty, that maybe the judges might find her lacking.

At the end of the week, the Dean of Music summoned her for a conference. "Sit down, Virginia," Dean Wallace said. A handsome man with salt-and-pepper hair and thick glasses, his smile instantly put her at ease. He began in a slight southern drawl. "I hope you like our campus." She nodded timidly. "I know you have your heart set on becoming a piano major, Virginia, but I want to point out a few hard facts of life. There really isn't much of a future in concert piano. Many gifted pianists are going hungry because of the competition from records and television. These days not many people are willing to pay to hear a pianist at a live concert. It's sad, but true."

"But it has always been my dream to be a concert pianist," she began.

He shook his head. "You must be realistic, Virginia, and you do have other options. Teaching offers more financial security for a woman. May I suggest you consider Choral Education?"

She saw her dream begin to dissipate and asked, "But why choral music? I've never taken voice lessons or sung a solo."

"That's why you go to school, Virginia, to learn these disciplines. There is little security in teaching piano privately in your home. With a Choral Music degree you can teach in schools, earn a salary that includes all the benefits. These days it is vital to have that coverage." He sounded like Myreeg, who always warned her to be practical in matters of money. Believing the Dean knew what he was talking about, Virginia switched concentration to Choral Education. The acceptance to the School of

Music had materialized but not in a manner that Virginia had hoped.

By the time Orientation Week was over, Virginia was homesick. The newness of being away from family, coupled with the independence that went with it, wore off with each passing day. Michael seemed to sense this when talking to her over the phone that first weekend, and he and Victoria resolved to visit as often as possible.

Over dinner one Saturday night at the Pretzel Bell, the three would talk of Virginia's studies and life on campus amid nearby students at other tables laughing and drinking big pitchers of beer.

"I had no idea it would be this hard," Virginia said over a stein of beer. "I'm not as prepared as the students from New York and Europe; they have musical backgrounds in conducting, theory, and composition. And..." she leaned closer and added, "I'm kind of lonely. Don't know anyone."

Michael patted Virginia's hand. "Don't worry about competition from the other students. You smart girl. Have courage, you catch up."

"Vehrsheen," Victoria added, "iss hard for you now, because iss first time you away from home. As a child, I was always alone. Most of my life I live with strangers. I hated that. Now you are lonely. But you have a mother and father who care about you. Like your father say, you can do it."

Virginia listened to her with fascination; it was the first time Myreeg had shown any warmth toward her.

Although the frequent visits from Michael and Victoria helped, Virginia continued to be lonely. After a few weeks she started to lose interest in studying and practicing; these had always been tactics to evade Myreeg, but now with her away, Virginia lost the motivation. More attention was instead focused toward altering her habits of shrinking from people and overeating, which brought the resolve to make major life changes by unlocking repressed feelings.

It started with practical jokes on fellow dorm inhabitants, jokes which often brought attention and amusement from the other girls. One of her favorite pranks involved slipping into other rooms while the occupants were in class, and short-sheeting the beds. A little "crunch" was added by sprinkling corn flakes in between the sheets. Oh, the enjoyment that came from hearing the squeals that rang up and down the hall when the girls returned. Other times she and Valerie would knock on a girl's door, and whoever answered got a faceful of shaving cream. The girls in the dorm would laugh but Virginia sensed from their questionable glances they looked down at her.

After the midnight curfew each Saturday night, the girls would gather in one room to describe their dates. They would giggle over the dumb things each guy had said, the unique ways he tried to "score." One guy had asked Elaine if he might borrow a quarter to call his mom, as she had instructed him to call her when he was in love. This brought out laughter and guffaws from the captive audience. Another girl had gone out with an Egyptian graduate engineer student, who spent much of his time kissing her between her right hand and shoulder, saying that her eyes resembled the stars. The room was divided over this encounter; some thought him to be a romantic while others found the actions to be only a ploy.

Fascinated by these tales Virginia risked ridicule one night by asking them to teach her how to kiss.

Maggie grabbed a pillow and handed it to Virginia. "Sure, there's nothing to it. Just pretend the pillow is Carl Collins—he's a handsome one. Now, put your lips together and pucker up, like this." Everyone laughed at the face Maggie made. "Take the pillow and try it. Go on."

Virginia looked around the room at the girls urging her on, laughing. "Okay, Carl, you lucky dog. You're really gonna get it!" She wrapped her arms around the pillow and buried her face in the middle.

"Hey," Maggie yelled after a minute. "Time to come up for air. You'll smother the poor guy."

The girls howled. Virginia hadn't really learned anything about kissing, but did learn not to ask stupid questions, especially in public.

*   *   *   *

College life had provided the freedom to say whatever she pleased without being censored by Myreeg. She talked volubly about everything—music, books, professors, classes, politics, religion—to anyone within earshot. Her grades, however, began to suffer. She scrambled to prepare for exams late into the night before, drinking mugs of coffee and smoking cigarettes to stay awake. Her first-term grades were subsequently so low that she was placed on academic probation, with risk of flunking out and disappointing herself and her parents.

The time for silliness was over.

Chapter 10

Michael and Victoria had told Virginia over and over that romance was very different from love. Romance was superficial, it was the flirting and playing games, all the things that men and women did before deciding to make a serious commitment. Romance existed when the relationship was happy, but disappeared at the first sign of conflict. Love, by comparison, was a solid commitment which bound two people together through good and bad times. According to Myreeg, someone who loved did not need the games of romance to determine their commitment. The commitment had already been formed without regard to character or appearance. To the Armenian culture love was a commitment—they did not need courting, flirting or dating to gauge their compatibility, rather both had the determination to remain loyal to the other and together raise a family which would honor the Armenian values which they themselves held sacred.

Michael had often said, "Good people come from good families. When you buy a dog you look at the pedigree and you know how it's gonna turn out. That goes for people, too. Vehrsheen, you find a good husband by looking at his parents. Dating is a waste of time."

Victoria added, "That's how we got together, your father and me. This talk about romance means nothing. Americans say I love you, I love you, kiss, kiss, kiss, and when one little thing goes wrong...divorce. Easy way out."

Virginia clamped her lips together. There was no sense arguing with their dating edict, as it was unlikely they would ever think differently. To her, romance was as important as love; it was an avenue for preventing commitment to a stranger. The thought of marrying without previous involvement seemed a reckless move and more than a little horrifying. "Just because a guy's parents are good people doesn't make him good," she thought.

Still, it was impossible to shake off the family taboo about romance, dating and love. Evenings in front of the dorm, Virginia witnessed boys and girls holding hands, embracing and kissing goodnight. She was embarrassed to watch, but secretly wished to do the same without guilt or inhibition. Occasionally someone asked her on a date but each time they were politely turned away, because Virginia had no idea how to act on a date, nor how to show interest in a man. Other girls flirted with ease in the company of a handsome man, but they were all experienced. She wanted that experience and yet at the same time wanted to avoid embarrassment which would certainly follow from inexperience. There was also loyalty to Myreeg and Hyreeg, who both adamantly insisted that dating was unnecessary. Saturday nights were thus spent alone studying.

Late one October afternoon the buzzer rang twice in Virginia's room. One buzz meant the phone, two buzzes meant a visitor. No visitors were expected. Upon reaching the lobby she approached an unfamiliar young man, who smiled as she appeared from the elevator.

"Virginia?" he asked.

"Yes?"

"My name's Tom," he said, extending his hand. "I'm a reporter from the Michigan Daily, the school newspaper. We're doing a survey about dating on campus. Would you mind if I asked you a few questions?"

"Questions about what?"

"Well, for example, the type of men you like to date, and whether you go on blind dates, that sort of thing."

"You're getting rather personal. Are you sure you're from the Michigan Daily?"

His face turned red and he burst into laughter. "I've been found out," he said. "Actually, I'm Armenian too, and I just used the Daily as a gimmick to meet you."

When she did not reply, he continued. "I was looking through the Student Directory and your name ended with an *ian*, so I assumed you were Armenian. Can you sit and talk for awhile?"

Smiling, she nodded. "Let's go into the living room and talk. We've probably got a lot in common."

They sat on the couch for over an hour, talking excitedly about their school and families. Tom was from Detroit, the second son in a family of three boys; as a junior he was planning to major in psychology. Virginia spoke of Myreeg and Hyreeg, the shoe shop and Johnny's stint at Fort Knox and how he'd moved back to Pontiac and gotten married. At the end of their talk Tom stood to leave. A short silence followed whereupon Tom tapped his brow three times before saying, "Would you want to see a movie with me on Sunday at three p.m.?" Virginia smiled, nodded and said that would be fun.

On Saturday she went shopping at Jacobson's for suitable first-date apparel. Within an hour she bought a brown tweed jumper, yellow turtle-neck top, and leather pumps.

That Sunday, in energetic anticipation, she dressed four hours early. During the wait she compiled a mental list of conversational topics while practicing to walk in the new pumps, not ever having walked in elevated shoes. At three o'clock exactly the buzzer rang twice. Not wanting to appear overly eager, she forced herself to wait two minutes before taking the elevator downstairs to the lobby where Tom awaited near the reception desk.

"Hi, Virginia." He smiled, taking her arm. "My, you look nice." He paused to catch his breath and then said, "The movie is *On The Waterfront* with Marlon Brando."

"That won four Academy Awards, didn't it?"

"Yes...shall we go? It will take us half an hour to walk there."

Walking to the U of M Theatre, Virginia felt as though on stilts. It was difficult to walk straight and concentrate on what Tom was saying, as most of her attention was devoted to walking naturally in elevated pumps. In reality it was obvious she never wore them before in her life. By the time they got to the movie she was exhausted, blisters already forming on her heels and feet.

Sitting beside a man in a darkened theatre was distracting to the point where Virginia was unable to pay any attention to Marlon Brando. How should she react if Tom attempted to hold her hand or put his arm around her shoulders? Should she allow him, or politely turn away? In the end it really didn't matter because he attempted neither. Ever-present feelings of self consciousness and worthlessness came flooding back after the movie; his actions seemed to suggest she was not attractive.

The walk back to the dorm was quiet, Virginia convinced this was to be her last date. Tom occasionally attempted to break the stand of silence, usually commenting on the movie. Virginia only nodded her head, too lost in her rejection. Arriving back at the dorm, however, he said, "I had a good time, Virginia. Let's have dinner at The Bell next Saturday."

Eyes widened. "Well...Tom," she began, "I was planning to go to an art show that night, but I'd like to have dinner some other night." Tom smiled and suggested the time. She agreed and said goodnight, skipping all the way to the elevator after making certain he was out of sight.

Over the next few months Tom and Virginia "kept company." She felt safe with a fellow Armenian; there was an unspoken understanding that he would not make any ungentlemanly advances toward her. As the months went by, however, she actually wished Tom would make advances, to take the initiative and perhaps soundly kiss her. But she couldn't bring herself to hint or issue the slightest invitation for intimacy. There was the reality that she still didn't know how to kiss despite the pillow lessons, and the embarrassment was too great, keeping her from acting on any feelings for Tom.

After six months Tom stopped calling.

*   *   *   *

One cold March day during the following semester Virginia returned to the dorm after finishing a difficult Theory exam in music, looking forward to a quiet afternoon to unwind. The buzzer rang once. She raced through the corridor to the telephone.

"Hi, Virginia, this is Grant Sarkisian. Missed you in English class today."

"I'm down in the dumps, Grant. I'm sure I've failed my Theory exam."

"I've got just the medicine for you, Virginia.   Let's drive out to Silver Lake. That should pick up your spirits."

Silver Lake was fifteen miles north of Ann Arbor. It had the reputation around campus for being a romantic spot. Virginia was dubious about the two of them being at the lake together in mid-winter; Myreeg's words of disapproval roared back to memory: "Only street girls sit in a car alone with a boy."

But Grant was Armenian, outspoken and of friendly demeanor. He would be just the person to raise her spirits.

"All right, Grant. I'll be ready in half an hour."

He picked her up and together they drove down a narrow road where snow was piled high against the banks and long icicles hung from the trees. Light reflected from the smooth ice of the lake. Virginia laughed at Grant's struggles to avoid fishtailing the car into drifts; his face was animated and eyes showed great amusement.

"If we get stuck you'll have to carry me back to Ann Arbor on your shoulder," she teased.

"I'll just make a sled out of the spare tire and pull you. You'll get a free ride."

Both were completely at ease when Grant pulled the car into a secluded area. Virginia started to shake as he moved close enough for her to feel his body temperature. He leaned over and kissed her, sending off alarms in her head, Myreeg's voice coming back with the stern warning that, "If a man is really serious about a girl he won't touch her before marriage."

"Grant," she whispered, pushing him away, "don't."

"Please, Virginia, just one more kiss."

"No! Stop now. I think I should be getting home."

He leaned back against his seat, looking at the floor and shaking his head. "I'm sorry, Virginia, I didn't mean to scare you. I'll take you home now."

During the silent ride back to the dorm Virginia sat with arms folded across her chest thinking of how proud Myreeg would be.

Chapter 11

The short, plump, henna-haired Voice professor, Miss Libby, pushed her pupil relentlessly to improve soprano range and produce a pleasant sound, ignoring the fact that Virginia was an alto. She'd press one fist against Virginia's abdomen, the other against her jaw, shouting harshly, "Will you never learn! You must breathe with your diaphragm. Relax your throat and round your vowel sounds."

Virginia trembled and perspired, her low range strained to attain the high notes Miss Libby demanded. Each successive attempt produced only high pitched squeaks which in turn seemed to encourage Miss Libby to push further. After each lesson Virginia left the studio feeling as if a bulldozer had flattened her.

Her best friend in the music school was Sharon Connelly, a born soprano who sang in clear bell-like tones but was a mere novice when it came to playing the piano. They spent hours together practicing, Sharon teaching Virginia how to relax her voice and Virginia showing Sharon simplified chords for piano accompaniment.

The two lived in the same dorm and often walked to class together, but Virginia did not see Sharon socially, as Sharon was usually away with her boyfriend and Virginia was busy with studies. Yet the two shared a common appreciation for music, especially classical works. Sharon understood Virginia's frustrations with the voice lessons and specifically the conflict with Miss Libby, and was sympathetic.

Near the end of the second semester, after a particularly wrenching session, Virginia came storming out shouting, "I can't take anymore! I quit!"

Sharon, who was waiting outside the door, rushed to Virginia and put her arm around her. They walked together through the Arcade, crossed State Street to the "Diag" to sit on a cement bench. "What's wrong, Ginny? Trouble with the stupid voice teacher?"

"What else? She's giving me a 'D', Sharon. I'm quitting. This time I'm serious. I can't learn anything from her. The bitch hates me and I hate her! Here, read this letter:"

February 1, 1955
University of Michigan
School of Music
Ann Arbor

Miss Virginia Haroutunian
546 Mosher Hall
Ann Arbor, Michigan

Dear Miss Haroutunian,

Attached you will find your transcript giving your record to date in the undergraduate division of the School of Music. You have been placed on academic probation until such time that you satisfy the 2.0 or C average. Note under Faculty Action, <u>needs counseling</u>.

Sincerely yours,

Sally Monsour

Sharon read and mumbled. "You can't let one negative teacher get to you like this. You're doing well in all your other subjects. Concentrate on your goal and just tough it out."

"But she just doesn't seem to appreciate the effort I've made to learn voice. My goal when I came here was to play the piano, but they told me to switch to voice. I've never sung seriously in my life, never considered myself ever to be a vocalist. I took their advice in good faith thinking it was possible to learn to sing and all I get is constant negativity. How can I possibly be expected to learn something if there is always such a high degree of tension each time I go to my lesson?"

Sharon shook her head. "She just doesn't realize how much time you put into your practicing. Keep at it. Maybe you won't have to listen to Miss Libby for more than a term. Maybe you could change tutors, get someone who's as good as Miss Libby is bad. Stay with it—success and progress are never handed to you." She playfully nudged Virginia's arm. "You've got to keep giving long after the energy burns out."

Virginia pondered Sharon's advice and remembered the Dean of Women's remarks from Orientation Day about persistence and tune-ups. This was a time to make repairs, so to speak. Further, Hyreeg and Myreeg would be disappointed if she gave up. With renewed zest and determination she continued the lessons.

The School of Music required that students remain assigned to the same Voice teacher, yet the following semester Virginia was assigned someone new. Sharon had gone in confidence to Dean Wallace and described Virginia's frustrations over the tutorial, saying that the near result was a resolve to quit college. Instead of the "bulldozer," Virginia now had a patient professor in Miss Greer, a former Metropolitan Opera star.

In preparation for the final exam at the end of fall semester junior year, Virginia met with the kindly Miss Greer.

"Let's face it, Virginia, you're never going to be another opera star like Beverly Sills. But you have the skills, personality and enthusiasm to be eminently qualified to teach music, history, theory, piano and to conduct choral groups. You have a find career ahead of you."

Virginia nodded. She basked in the confidence and encouragement given by Miss Greer, which helped propel her to a B in Voice for junior year. For the final solo she selected *"Seeroon Manushag"* (Sweet Violet) in a range suitable to her voice. Most of the songs in Music School were performed in German or Italian, but Miss Greer suggested the old Armenian folk tune instead, saying that the Jury would never know the difference. Indeed this was

quite true. The Jury was enamored with the piece, enthusiastic that Virginia had attempted something different.
With that final solo she completed all requirements for the
undergraduate degree in music.   Her senior year was
focused on student teaching between grades K-12. In 1958
she graduated from the University of Michigan with high
honors and numerous accomplishments, and yet still
prudish and lonely.

                        *   *   *   *

        Virginia obtained her first job teaching choir at a
high school in Belleville, Michigan.   Suffering through the
normal trials of the first job, she worked at becoming
familiar with the school rules, adjusting to all the students
and getting to know the faculty. She settled into a shared
apartment with three girlfriends from college, on weekends
returning to Myreeg and Hyreeg to assist with the moderately successful shoe shop.
        Virginia taught for two years without any major
change.   Despite living in Ann Arbor, fifty miles from
Myreeg and Hyreeg, their influence over her was always
evident.   Instead of looking forward to her own future of
perhaps raising family, Virginia instead remained focused
toward Hyreeg and Myreeg, in many ways still the child
that hadn't yet grown to adulthood. Their decisions were
still final to her; she obeyed loyally and without question.
Yet in her consciousness a growing sense of unhappiness
emerged.   Girlfriends were getting married, traveling and
having children while her life remained unchanged.   The
desire for independence and direction propelled her to seriously ponder the possibility of moving to California where
the distance might give the needed emancipation and
ability to act upon her own thoughts rather than the
counsel of Myreeg and Hyreeg.   Résumés were sent, and
before the end of the 1960 school year an offer came from
the Santa Barbara Public Schools.
        "California, here I come," she sang after reading the
offer. A quick acknowledgment confirmed her interest and
the following day Belleville was advised she would not be
returning.

During the summer hiatus lists were made of clothes to take, maps to examine, places to visit and so forth. She and her housemate, Margo, spent many late nights anticipating a life out West. Margo, who was soon to marry Saul, another close friend, advised Virginia on methods for reading men and how to determine their interest and then act upon it. Virginia grew more enthusiastic as the time to leave approached. There was one final detail, however: she hadn't told Myreeg and Hyreeg.

During a warm August Sunday afternoon over shish ka bob and pilaf she blurted the news. "I'm moving to California to take a job teaching in the Santa Barbara Public Schools. I leave at the end of the month."

Michael's face turned pink. "Move to California?" he cried. "That's ridiculous! Biggest mistake of your life."

"You can't go away, Vehrsheen," Myreeg exclaimed. "You keep running back to us every weekend now. You be lost all alone in that big state...impossible!"

"That's exactly my point. I must get away and be on my own."

Michael shook his head. "I don't understand that talk. You have everything you need to make you happy right here."

"I'm twenty-four years old and not on my own. I've got to grow up."

Victoria threw her napkin on the table. "Iss crazy talk. You don't make sense, Vehrsheen." Grumbling, she cleared the table. "So what iss different? I work and slave for you to go away and leave us alone. Johnny busy with his family. Don't see him much. Just wait...in three, four weeks you be back. Waste all that money for nothing."

Within the week Virginia canceled the trip.

*   *   *   *

With the school year set to begin Virginia was without a job and deeper in the very life she sought to flee. A college classmate eased some of the worries by finding a job teaching music at a junior high school in Pontiac. But there was another conflict: where to live. Margo had moved to New York to be with Saul in anticipation of their marriage. She had no one with whom to sublet an apartment, and Myreeg constantly berated her, saying, "Nice girls don't live in apartment alone." Thus Virginia moved back home.

She once again had to prove her teaching credibility to the Pontiac faulty and student body, teaching all aspects of music from theory to composers, to history and appreciation. In the spring of 1961 she motivated many of her ninth grade choral vocalists to participate in a production of *My Fair Lady*. The classes worked from January to May mastering all the complexities and nuances of the show. When it went up before the school in the spring, the two night performances packed the auditorium. The idea of having a choral group act as well as sing impressed students, faculty, and parents; thus Virginia's creative teaching methods brought notoriety within the social circle of fellow teachers.

With Virginia's entrance into the social scene at school, she was privy to all the gossip and talk among the teachers. Other teachers noticed there was never any gossip about Virginia, and upon learning that she was unattached, frequently offered to arrange dates. Each time Virginia would have ready a clever excuse that hinted at an ever active social life. No one suspected the bluff.

Virginia was healthy, had a good rewarding career with no financial burdens, and yet loneliness still overwhelmed her. There was a constant struggle to fill empty leisure hours. She volunteered to be music librarian for the Pontiac Symphony, taught Sunday School at the Armenian church and took graduate music classes. Each time another girlfriend married or had a baby Virginia had to find another activity to fend off renewed bouts of depression stemming from a feeling of isolation.

In the summer of 1961 she left for Spain to visit newlyweds Margo and Saul, who were living off a scholarship.

Chapter 12

Saul had been awarded a Tiffany Grant, which allowed him to study in Spain for the 1960-1961 school year. He and Margo were happily married, both finding Spain to be the ideal setting for his art and her writing. Their correspondence to Virginia detailed freedom in and exposure to the unfamiliar culture and landscape, leaving her envious. Letters came back describing friendly Spaniards from villages near Barcelona who often indiscriminately invited Margo and Saul to join in drink while they played classical guitar or danced to the flamenco.

At Christmas Virginia received a letter Margo had written from Barcelona.

> "We're so happy Ginny. We want to share our joy with you. Start planning now for a two month visit with us next summer. Saul says don't bring a lot of luggage if you don't want to carry it. You'll really enjoy Spain."

> Love,

> Margo

Virginia started saving money for what seemed only a fantasy. She told Myreeg and Hyreeg the travel plans, to which they protested vigorously at her flying alone to a foreign country, insisting that she go with a group instead. Their stories of foreign visitors being robbed by unscrupulous cab drivers and street merchants, being left in a foreign territory without money or passport, left Virginia feeling trepid.   Despite this grim portrayal of Spain, however, she still remained firm in her resolve to visit Margo and Saul, who had found the country beautiful and friendly; so perhaps Myreeg and Hyreeg were not fully informed.   How could they possibly know a land they'd never visited themselves?   She proceeded with plans to leave the day after school finished for the summer.

Myreeg and Hyreeg drove Virginia to Metropolitan Airport on June 14, suggesting that it was not too late for her to back out.   When she didn't, they gave her last minute safety advice before wishing safe passage and good health.   Virginia boarded the plane wondering what to expect from Spain, its culture and its men.   Having trusted Margo and Saul with arranging all the activities, she only needed to sit back and let things fall as they might.   The plane taxied down the runway and began a smooth ascension toward New York's LaGuardia.   After landing in New York Virginia had only a few moments to catch her connecting flight to Barcelona.   The seven hour journey over the Atlantic passed slowly with Virginia unable to sleep, anxious of the possibilities in Spain.   The plane landed in Barcelona early the next morning on what looked to be a cow pasture—a strip of cement surrounded by green grass and weeds.   No buildings or people were in visual range, only an old rusted double-deck bus sat parked in the field.   The bus transported passengers to the terminal, a small, single storey building filled with Spanish advertisements and announcements bellowing over a loudspeaker of arriving and departing flights.   At first Virginia did not see Margo or Saul amid the bustling crowds of Spaniards, but as she walked toward an airline information desk, a familiar voice beckoned above the crowd, "Ginny! Ginny!" Virginia saw Margo and Saul both elbowing above the congested area, waving.   They nudged their way to each other and embraced.   Virginia said, "Margo I thought you'd forgotten about me."

"We're sorry, Ginny. We're late because of the rush hour traffic."

Saul carried her luggage to the car.   "Why all the suitcases, Ginny? We're going to be moving around quite a bit. I'll carry it for you this time, but on the trip everyone carries their own weight." They ushered Virginia to a new white Renault. Margo explained, "We got it in London. Our friend Eileen helped us arrange to get it cheaply. You'll get to meet her actually, she's going to tour with us. Talks a lot but says intelligent things. You'll like her. Lots of fun. Besides, that allows us to split the expenses four ways. We'll meet her back at the pensión in a little while."

Throughout the drive Virginia observed the landscape, surprised to see goats and donkeys freely roaming the streets and stopping traffic. "Wouldn't this be a comical sight in America?" she thought. "I can picture Americans blowing their horns impatiently, waiting for a goat to cross the freeway."

"Ginny," said Margo, interrupting her observations. "You needn't worry about anything. I have completely mapped out our itinerary. All you have to do is come along for the ride, relax and enjoy."

"Let me warn you ahead of time, Ginny," cautioned Saul. "Margo and I are living on a two thousand dollar scholarship for one year in Spain. I suppose you saved a lot of money, but we have to pinch our pennies and stick to our budget. That means no elegant restaurants." He smiled.

"Oh, I don't mind, Saul...I'll go anywhere you go."

They laughed and Saul continued. "We'll rise at four o'clock in the morning when we drive to another town, the reason being to avoid traveling during the hottest part of the day. We stop at noon for siesta time. All the stores close and the workers go home to rest, returning to work by four. During that time we can find a shady place in the park by the fountain, drink wine and play pinochle."

"You'll love Spain, Ginny," purred Margo.

When they arrived at the pensión Virginia was introduced to Eileen, who spoke in a fast cockney dialect. She was tall and stocky, a large rounded face and hair pulled tightly back into a bun so that her entire forehead was visible. Margo's description of her was on target—she began talking the moment they arrived.

"I picked up the tickets for the bullfight this afternoon," she said. "After lunch let's try to leave early so we can get good seats. The bullfighters are staying in this very pensión. It'll be a thrill to see them in person."

The four of them walked into the pensión eatery,
which lacked any extravagance and decor; it was simply
several brown wooden tables and cracked chairs. A strong
scent of olive oil permeated through the eatery, causing
Virginia to lose her appetite. A waiter soon appeared and
took their orders; Virginia only nodded her head, as if to
say she'd have the same as everyone else. The waiter
started to bring out food immediately after placing the
orders—first came flattened fried eggs, then salad, followed
by *paella*, a rice dish with pimentos and shrimp. Finally
the lunch was served—fish with *sangria*. Virginia, unac-
customed to such large meals and still feeling sick from the
overpowering stench of olive oil, politely explained to the
curious waiter that she was not hungry.

Before finishing the meal, a line of bullfighters
dressed in full attire walked down the hotel staircase and
entered the eatery. Eileen cheered loudly, jumping to her
feet and seizing Margo's camera to snap a picture of the
amused men. Virginia, embarrassed by Eileen's fawning
and cooing over the men, pretended to be too interested in
her food to notice.

They left for the bullfight shortly following lunch,
finding seats in the sun section, the cheapest. Virginia
disliked sitting in the 110° unshaded area but said nothing
as everyone else seemed content.

The trumpets heralded the opening of the show. A
parade of bullfighters marched around the arena and
stopped in front of the dignitary's box where the mayor sat.
They presented him with flowers before marching off the
field, signaling readiness to begin the match. A beautiful
tan bull was released from the pen, running immediately to
the center, bucking its head and tail. The *banderilero*
emerged calling and teasing the bull, holding a large
banderilla firmly in each hand to pick the bull in the back
as he ran past.

Margo and Saul stood up cheering, joining the entire
crowd in shouting "*olé*" in unison, waving white handker-
chiefs in the air. Virginia sat in disbelief over her friends'
acceptance of what she deemed brutal behavior. She'd
never seen Margo so animated over such a spectacle of

violence; at home, Margo would never watch football because of its brutality.

Next the *picador* appeared, sitting on a horse covered in padding to ensure that the horns of the bull did not penetrate. He rode past the bull, aiming his lance at the back of the animal's neck to ensure the head would be kept low for subsequent stages. Margo leaned over the Virginia and said, "If a bull knocks the *picador* and horse down, the audience will "boo" the *picador* off the field like a bad actor."

Finally the *toreador* appeared with red cape draped over his sword. He beckoned the bull, now weak from bleeding and very angry, and prepared for the finale. The bull charged as the *toreador* confidently waved him through his cape. After several attempts at getting the *toreador*, the bull stopped, panting and staring. The *toreador* took out his sword and expertly ran the bull through, inserting at the neck and killing him instantly. Margo told Virginia that if the *toreador* failed to kill the bull, the butcher must come out and end the bull's suffering.

The bull died amid heavy cheering. The butcher emerged with a dagger type blade to cut off the ears, handing them to the *toreador*, who took the offering and paraded about the arena, accepting applause and a showering of flowers with long deep bows. Meanwhile, the carcass was attached to a team of horses and dragged away. Groundskeepers raked over the bloody areas to prepare for the next match.

Virginia cried when the bull was killed. "I can't stand this sport, Margo. It's so brutal."

"It seems cruel at first, Ginny," Margo said. "But in reality it isn't. The death is inevitable, you know, and the bulls lead very good lives while being carefully groomed, being treated like high royalty. The people here respect the bull, they look upon it with honor."

The next round began and the cheering and chanting resumed. With each subsequent match Virginia grew more entranced by the entire scene; the process and artistry which each bullfighter took to command the bull, the sheer courage with which they called upon to grapple with such an enormous yet majestic animal. Virginia saw a people engaged so closely to a sport which emphasized honor, respect, strength and courage. It was more than mere violence; it was a display of heroism, strength, calculation and even a touch of charisma. The bullfighters indeed respected the bull, making sure that they did not unduly cripple him so that he might not be able to defend himself. Whenever a bull was dishonored by a fighter the crowd would explode in catcalls. Also, if the bull dishonored the fighter, the fighter was considered weak and a failure.

After the final fight they left the arena and walked back to the pensión.

"I forgot to tell you, Ginny," said Margo. "We don't eat dinner until nine o'clock here. And what's so beautiful is that we sit at outdoor cafés under the moonlit sky and stars. It's very romantic."

"I'd love that." Virginia smiled.

"I'm hungry," Eileen chanted. "Let's stop at a café for a *tapas*."

"A *tapas*?" Virginia asked.

"Small appetizers of shrimp, escargot or octopus in garlic sauce. Delicious," informed Eileen.

"No thanks," Virginia exclaimed. "You won't talk me into eating those strange looking things."

"Still a picky eater, eh?" Saul teased. "I remember those days in Michigan when all you'd eat is shish ka bob and pilaf. Experiment, Virginia, try new foods. You might like them. There are other foods besides those which your mother makes."

They stopped at a sidewalk café and watched the people walk past. Eileen had her *tapas* and Virginia tried some octopus, which she did not like.

After the *tapas*, Margo and Saul took Virginia to Güell park where Antoni Gaudí had used broken cups with saucers and blue glass from rosewater bottles for mosaic designs on the pavilion, the serpentine benches and fountain; Saul said the park was a failed high-income housing project that was donated to the city of Barcelona by Güell, a noted developer, who hired Gaudí to design the layout of the park. Virginia was astounded by the number of broken pieces of cups and saucers Gaudí had used in his artwork and the length of time it must have taken to design and assemble.

They followed a narrow winding road down to the Sagrada Familia, Gaudí's unfinished cathedral. The architecture was very unusual with its spires resembling organ pipes, which seemed to reach toward the heavens.

On the bus ride back to their hotel, Saul pointed out the Casa Míla, a gigantic apartment building which resembled sea cliffs; made of stone and steel with iron balconies, it was another noted creation by Gaudí. The huge stone chimneys looked like centurions wearing helmets, looking as if to guard the fortress from enemy invaders. While observing, Virginia thought Gaudí belonged in the great family of geniuses the like of Bach, Beethoven and Toscanini. His works were as creative, unique and brilliant as any artist, she'd never seen any design quite like his.

After four days in Barcelona Virginia and her friends traveled to Madrid. Her first observation was a flea market, the largest she'd ever seen. In 100° weather she watched elderly men carry rusty drain pipes and parts from old machinery down the street on their backs, all of which would be considered junk in America. A gypsy woman browsed while breast-feeding an infant. Virginia wandered through the various tents which exhibited secondhand jewelry, housewares and furniture, but saw no reason to spend money, instead interested more in the faces and dialect that floated spontaneously throughout almost giving the impression of being on a movie set.

Following the visit to the Flea Market, Saul led the three women to the Prado Museum to observe the artwork of Goya, one of his favorites. They walked through the grandiose museum, noticing the effort and detail of each work but being careful not to ask any questions, as he was absorbed in appreciation and did not like to be interrupted...much like a musician enjoying an opera. Virginia was too engrossed anyway with the knowledge that she was observing internationally renowned work in a museum considered throughout the world to be one of the finest.

The world began to feel boundless to her while gazing at the works. There was so much more to be seen outside of everyday life in Pontiac. While contemplating the works she suddenly felt liberated in the sense that she was witnessing activities and ideas which were unavailable within the confines of Pontiac. The difference in culture, and the way Spaniards interacted with one another and the way in which they expressed ideas was fascinating. There was more emotion and passion within them, more of a willingness to take risks. Pontiac, by comparison, was a remote little area making up only a piece of a much larger puzzle; her friends at home had one objective for their entire life—one job which they did for their livelihood, never leaving, never exploring. There was so much more to see, so much more to experience outside of everyday surroundings. There were other peoples to know from places far beyond Pontiac. New perspectives and insights were to be gained from these people; new philosophies, other than those of Myreeg and Hyreeg. Artists such as Goya had independently developed their own ideas, philosophies and dreams and had shaped their vision from their own singular observations and experiences. All of Virginia's ideas, by comparison, were an outgrowth of Myreeg and Hyreeg, her ideas had been shaped around their observations and experiences. Her actions were always in accordance with their conclusions. There was a sudden recognition that had she obeyed their wishes to cancel the visit to Spain, all of these observations would surely have been lost.

But what of loyalty? Myreeg and Hyreeg were her family, and she loved them and was loyal to them always. Over the years she strove to make them proud by doing their will, and yet each time she grew more and more unhappy. How was this possible, to be happy for disregarding them, and yet wanting desperately to remain loyal?

Margo noted Virginia's fascination with Goya's work and whispered to her, "You ain't seen nothin' yet. Wait 'til we get to Pamplona. You'll see why Hemingway was so in love with Spain."

After a week in Madrid the four ventured to Pamplona where they rented rooms from a Spanish family. Every morning Saul made arrangements for their dinners to be prepared by a restaurateur down the street. Annually, beginning on the 7th of July, the Pamploneses celebrated for one week their fiestas in honor of San

Fermin.   There were dancers, prayers, bullfights, songs
depicting anguished moments of the *encierros*; all of these
showing the sincerity and spontaneity of the people and
illustrating their strong affinity for tradition and the past.
At five a.m. that first morning in Pamplona the four gathered in the town square facing city hall, a two storey stone
building, to watch the clock tower. A cannon fired once to
signal the start of the fiesta. The clock rang six bells and
the mayor announced over the loudspeaker in Spanish,
"Pamploneses! Pamploneses! From this moment on begins
the fiesta of the Patron Saint. May St. Fermin give his
greatest blessings to all. Long live St. Fermin!" he shouts.
The crowd echoes, "Long live St. Fermin!" Canons shoot
off; masses of people cheer in the streets and squares;
brass bands of Pamplona play Spanish marches; men
dressed in white shirts and red scarves dance about the
streets. A parade with eight giant replicas of heroes and
saints pass by, all with huge ceramic heads.

At sundown that evening Margo, Saul, Virginia and
Eileen lined up next to a wooden barricade to guarantee
visibility for the infamous bull run at four a.m. the
following morning. At the break of dawn the weary crowd
of onlookers stirred as several gunshots were fired in the
air to signal the runners to begin running before the bulls
were released.   The angry animals, prodded by trained
handlers, rampaged through the barricaded streets chasing
madly after the crowd of literally thousands running ahead.
Virginia watched from behind the safety of the fences at
those scurrying about madly to escape the bulls, many of
them jumping the temporary wooden gates or falling into
the streets, or being trampled by runners and or bulls.
Virginia marveled at the courage the men had to run in
front of angry bulls. By the end of the run one person had
been killed, several others had been injured.

That evening an American from Manhattan ate with
them at the restaurant and joined in conversation. Saul
talked to him about New York University, where they both
attended. When they finished and departed to find a place
to watch the fireworks, the American turned his attentions
to Virginia, who shared his interest in music.

The man from New York talked at length of the genius of Leonard Bernstein and how he had seen *West Side Story* in the city. Virginia told him she had directed that production and run into controversy with the musical supervisor, who believed the gangs and motorcycle jackets corrupted student minds. The American, Stan, shook his head saying it was outrageous. He shared similar stories which he'd observed, pausing long enough so that they might watch the fireworks. When the fireworks concluded he resumed storytelling.

Virginia shared Stan's passion for relating incidents of musical stupidity. However, after several minutes talking, she noticed Saul and Margo were not in view. At first she looked about the square without concern, but after five minutes when they did not appear she panicked, not remembering the name of the Spanish family nor their address. The American assured her that if Margo and Saul did not appear, he would not leave her unescorted in the city, that she was welcome to stay at his place. They walked to a bench in the central plaza and watched the faces entering and exiting until after midnight. Stan finally stood and said, "Let's go to my place." Virginia was apprehensive but had no alternative and agreed. Once at his flat Stan made several ungentlemanly advances, ignoring her orders to stop. Scared, she ran from his apartment into the street, where she stood several moments to ponder the next move. Meanwhile Stan emerged and said gruffly that he would drive her back to the plaza to wait for Margo and Saul. Plaza deserted, Stan left her at a bench and drove away hurriedly. Virginia sat hoping that Margo, Saul or Eileen might come, as it was two a.m. and they'd been separated for over three hours. About thirty minutes later the white Renault rolled around the corner and Margo jumped out screaming, "Where have you been? What happened? We were really nervous—we're on our way to the police."

Virginia told her about Stan.

"Let this be a lesson," said Saul sternly from behind the wheel of the Renault. "Don't get lost with strangers and always carry your address."

*   *   *   *

On Virginia's 25th birthday they drove down the streets lined with orange trees leading into Valencia. Virginia felt blue because she didn't let on that it was her birthday and no one had remembered. They checked into a pensión, took a swim in the Mediterranean, and saw a complete arching rainbow in the Sea. They returned and changed into dress clothes for dinner in the pensión. After the meal a waiter approached their table carrying a large white cake with twenty-five lighted candles; Virginia covered her reddening face. It was her first surprise party.

The ensuing weeks raced by with a whirl of color and beauty; Toledo, Córdoba, Granada and Cádiz. In Cádiz they met several bullfighters who were staying in the same pensión. Virginia became friendly with a *picador* named Angelo, who, after learning they were going to Seville as he was the following day, invited them all to see him fight. He rode horseback into the arena amid lively cheers. Virginia looked through her binoculars, recognizing him and shouting, "There's my *picador*, there's my *picador*." All the Spaniards understood her because of the similarity between my and the Spanish *mi*, so when the bull knocked Angelo and his horse down, all the Spaniards looked at her and laughed.

From Seville they drove up the Costa del Sol to the Rock of Gibraltar to see the wild apes. The mischievous apes were noted for jumping into open windows of cars and pilfering small objects like sunglasses or purses, which they would carry up to the tallest trees and drop into the ocean. Two Germans drove up on their motorcycles and parked aside the Renault, presumably to sightsee. When they left to walk, the apes tore the leather seats to shreds.

*   *   *   *

On the night before her departure for home, Virginia almost had a date. Margo and Saul took her to an exclusive restaurant, The Hogar Gallego, for a farewell dinner. They had a table in the outdoor café under the moon and stars, dining on escargot, paella, gazpacho, suckling pig and sangria. Beautiful guitar music floated through the air—a magical evening. In the middle of it a handsome Spaniard sitting alone at the next table leaned over and began talking to Virginia in Spanish. She asked Margo to translate.

"He's asking for permission to join us, Virginia. Is that agreeable with you?"

Virginia, flattered, answered shyly, "I suppose so." As he spoke, she sat dumbly, unable to understand a word and instead smiled vacantly to cover her ignorance.

Finally he turned to Margo. "Why is your friend so quiet? Is she a deaf mute?"

Everyone laughed except Virginia, who did not understand.

"She doesn't understand you," Margo explained. "She has studied Spanish but doesn't comprehend your dialect."

He turned to Virginia and smiled. "In that case, I would be delighted to give her lessons. Perhaps over dinner tomorrow?"

"That's very kind of you," Saul interrupted, "but Virginia is flying back to America tomorrow."

The man looked genuinely disappointed. "Oh, that's too bad." Then his eyes lit up. "How about breakfast?"

Margo turned to Virginia and smiled. "Would you care to have breakfast with this gentleman?"

After two months in Spain, finally a hint of romance.

"Yes, I would like that very much." She turned to the man and smiled, nodding. "Sí, Señor."

Arrangements were made for the two of them to meet at a small café near Virginia's pensión. The gentleman, Don José, bowed to them all and said goodnight. Virginia felt a bit giddy over this unexpected delight, and took leave of Margo and Saul to return to her room. She could not sleep; she hadn't been on a date since college three years before and worried that she was out of practice and also of the language difference. Don José had left the impression of a supreme gentleman and Virginia was concerned he might find her uninteresting. She grappled with all these thoughts much like a school girl, until finally falling asleep an hour before dawn.

She awoke at sunrise completely energetic. After meticulously preparing herself, she walked to the prearranged café near the town plaza, and sat at a sidewalk table to wait, ordering coffee with milk. Three cups of coffee later, Don José was nowhere to be seen. Hands over her cheeks, she stared into the empty coffee cup, saddened that such a gentleman as Don José would be so unkind. Yet a moment later, Margo came running through the plaza toward her. "Ginny, Don José just telephoned. He says he can't find you."

It turned out that she had been waiting outside the café under the hot sun while all the while Don José was downstairs inside the air-conditioned restaurant. When the two finally met they had a good laugh. It was too late for breakfast; Margo and Saul had already packed the Renault for the ride to the airport.

"We've still time for hurried coffee and a pastry," Don José suggested. "Then maybe we can take a stroll around the plaza."

And that was her bit of romance: coffee and pastry at a sidewalk café and then a leisurely promenade through Madrid's Plaza de Antonio. They had difficulty communicating with each other, but Virginia was thrilled when she was able to understand that he was asking for her address on a scrap piece of paper. "Maybe one day we'll meet again." He bowed.

Don José accompanied them all to the airport, helping to carry Virginia's luggage.

"We wish you'd change your mind, Ginny, and stay with us for a little longer," Margo said. "It's been wonderful having you."

"I'll never forget our memories of Spain," she promised. "Thank you for everything."

Margo and Saul both kissed her on each cheek. And then it was Don José's turn. Her heart fluttered as he leaned over and quickly kissed both cheeks.

"*Adiós,* Virginia. I will write to you." She smiled at him and waved a final goodbye to Margo and Saul before boarding the plane.

It was a fitting way to end those marvelous two months in Spain: a hint of romance. As her plane soared high into the skies, Virginia was once again filled with hope.

Chapter 13

Virginia lost her voice in mid April while shouting stage directions amid rehearsals for "Kismet." A specialist from the University of Michigan Hospital said her condition was an ailment common among people who spoke constantly. Virginia had a habit of continuing to speak when out of breath, which made the vocal cords rub together causing the development of polyps, and leaving her voice raspy and low. The doctor had prescribed complete voice rest for two months, which meant not even a whisper. Once the rest was complete she was to begin speech exercise to prevent reoccurrence. With two months left in the school year, she postponed the treatment and instead used a microphone during class, speaking only when necessary. When school finished in June, she began the voice rest, carrying pencil and paper wherever she traveled.

Most of the time was spent in the library, lost in the prose of Ayn Rand, D.H. Lawrence and Henry Miller. One afternoon while preparing to leave, a stack of books in her arms, she encountered a familiar young man. He recognized her instantly.

"Virginia Haroutunian? It is you! Do you remember me? Sean Gibson? I used to live a few doors away from you in Pontiac. We played roofball in junior high with the kids on the block."

A vision of the neighborhood kids tossing a handball onto a roof flashed into Virginia's head...especially the day this Sean had undershot the roof and the ball went through the front window. The kids had all scattered before Sean's grandmother came out to angrily survey the damage. Virginia wondered if his grandmother would ever

discover the true culprit.   Sean had visibly changed from
the mud-faced seventh grader whose specialty was
mischief, into a five-foot six handsome Danish blond
resembling Robert Stack in *The Untouchables*; he had
bright blue eyes that suggested a hint of the same
mischievous behavior which compelled him so in junior
high. With her pencil and pad,

   *"Yes, I remember you. Did you ever have to pay for
that window you broke?"*

   Sean grinned.   "Nobody squealed on me so Gram
never found out who did it. Started me on a life of lies and
deception for sure.   What's with the pencil and paper?
Laryngitis?"

   *"Doctor ordered me not to talk. I have to write every-
thing down on this pad."*

   He smiled.   "You're a pencil girl, eh?"   Virginia
looked to him in confusion, causing him to blush and look
to the ground in obvious embarrassment. Neither had any
idea of what was meant by being a "pencil girl."   Virginia
politely nodded and turned to walk home. Sean followed.
"You know, I work at a machine shop so I read engineering-
type books. And mysteries. What's your favorite?"

   "Best sellers and classics."

   "You've got quite a stack of books there. You must
read all the time."   Virginia shrugged.   He continued.   "I
just bought a new boat with a forty horsepower motor.
Would you like to go for a ride sometime?"

   Virginia stopped, recalling her near drowning at a
Methodist church camp, terrified of water ever since. She
wrote, *"No, thank you. I'm afraid of water."*

   "It's a very safe boat, Virginia.   And I'm a good
swimmer. If anything goes wrong I can rescue you."   He
laughed.   "I promise...no horseplay."

   She slowly nodded and wrote, *"All right. When?"*

   Sean clapped his hands together and suggested
tomorrow afternoon. She agreed and said goodbye, walking
home hurriedly and thinking how much Sean had changed
from the days as a rude, profane seventh grader. Walking
through the front door she found Myreeg in the living room
immersed in the headlines of the *Hairenik*. Virginia tapped
on the table to get her attention, then began writing on the

pad. *"I met Sean Gibson in the library today. Remember him? I'm going boating with him tomorrow."*

Myreeg stood, shaking her head. "No, you're not! We know that family. His parents are divorced. His mother leave him when he was baby and run around with other men. People say she drink too much."

"I don't care about his parents."

"He's been divorced too, Vehrsheen. You know your father won't let you date a divorced man."

"I'm just going out with a friend. Don't worry about it. Haireekeh."

The following day she went boating with Sean. In the middle of the lake he let her take the wheel while he gave navigational instructions, saying to steer into waves and avoid shallow waters. Nervous at first Virginia started slowly, but after Sean increased the speed she was exhilarated and insisted on increasing it further. For a few minutes the boat sped over the calm waters, running parallel to the smooth brown beaches filled to near capacity with vacationers. After several minutes Sean returned to the Captain's chair, cutting the engine and leaving the boat to drift. He offered Virginia a beer which she accepted. Leaning back in the Captain's chair, he opened a beer for himself.

"I belong to the Junior Chamber of Commerce, Virginia. The Jaycees are having a dinner dance next Saturday at the Veteran's Hall. Would you like to go with me?"

A smile and quick nod revealed her willingness. He smiled, drinking from his can of Miller.

So it was set. Two days prior to the dance she made a trip to the expensive designer dress shop, Hilda's, thinking this was a special occasion which warranted a little spending. One outfit seemed perfect: a white sheath dress. Perfect contrast to her bronzed skin. When trying it on she felt a wave of self-confidence; a year's worth of dieting and exercise yielded a trim and tanned figure which was perfectly displayed in the outfit. She was eager to show herself off.

Sean arrived on time, dressed in a light blue suit and white turtle neck, smiling. She brought him into the living room to introduce Myreeg and Hyreeg, who both sat reading. They looked long enough to nod at him without smiling and then resumed reading. Sean, unfazed by the lukewarm introduction, enthusiastically escorted Virginia to his car.

They arrived at the Veteran's Hall, decorated with crepe paper streamers and balloons, not unlike a high school gymnasium for a homecoming dance, and greeted a small crowd gathered outside watching the couples enter. Sean introduced Virginia and explained her voice problem.

"You don't need a voice, Virginia," one man said. "Your stunning dress says enough."

Virginia blushed as Sean led her off to the dance floor to move to such tunes as "Peppermint Twist," "The Limbo" and "Misty." After sweating it out on the floor, the two left amid enthusiastic applause to sit for dinner at a long table where several other couples were already eating. Sean, smiling broadly, leaned over to those beside him and spoke of how stunning Virginia looked and what a natural she was on the dance floor.

The evening concluded with several slow numbers. Virginia especially enjoyed "Smoke Gets In Your Eyes," as Sean danced close enough to suggest attraction and yet maintained a polite distance. When the music ended they said goodbye to the many well wishing admirers who nudged and winked at Sean as if to compliment his good taste in Virginia. Sean, in high spirits during the drive home, asked Virginia if they might picnic together on Labor Day. She nodded her head and wrote that she would make lunch for them.

On Labor Day Virginia was anxious for Sean to arrive; today he would hear her voice for the first time. He picked her up from the house and drove to the waterfront, where they unloaded the boat and cruised about the lake for an hour before Sean cut the engine to eat. Virginia took out her pad. *"Prepare yourself, Sean. I am about to speak."* She cleared her throat, drew in a deep breath and said, "The rine in spine sties minely on the pline."

He laughed heartily at the reference to Professor Higgins from *My Fair Lady.* "By Jove, she's got it! I've lost the Pencil Girl but gotten a Fair Lady."

Virginia tossed the old writing pad into the lake and using her regular voice, returned home at ten o'clock that night laughing. They said goodnight on her front steps under the glow of a street lamp. Sean slipped his arms around her, drawing close and kissing her. "Goodnight, Fair Lady," he whispered. Virginia held him for a long moment before pulling away suddenly, feeling that eyes were watching. "I had a wonderful time, Sean, but I must go in." He nodded and she turned to hurry inside.

Sure enough, her parents were watching in the foyer.

"Vehrsheen!" Hyreeg yelled angrily. "You won't see this divorced man again."

"Why? We're just friends."

"He's no good for you. He's divorced. His whole family drinks. You find someone from better family, find a nice Armenian man or stay where you belong."

Virginia ran to her bedroom and slammed the door. A moment later Myreeg quietly entered and sat beside her on the bed. "Vehrsheen, your father love you. He don't want you to get hurt. For your own good he say don't see him."

"I'm twenty-seven years old, Myreeg, and I'm lonely. All I do is work. A man is finally paying attention to me for the first time in my life and I like it. That doesn't mean I'll marry him. I just want to be with someone. I'm tired of being alone."

Myreeg stood and walked to the door to leave. "He is not right one for you, Vehrsheen. Better to be alone than married to the wrong man."

Chapter 14

Over the next year Sean and Virginia saw each other frequently; they boated together in the summer, golfed, bowled, saw horse races in Windsor, played cards and dined out on weekends. Eventually they were inseparable, which led friends to tease about possibilities of marriage. Hyreeg and Myreeg, however, persisted in their attempts to persuade Virginia to stop seeing Sean, refusing to allow him into their home.

The newness of having a companion wore off after the first year, as Virginia began to realize she had compromised her own interests to be with Sean. Music, her friends and theatre were all neglected for golf, bowling and horseracing. This all grew tiresome and Virginia resorted to deliberately picking fights with him in order to address the fact that Sean had no interest in any of her pursuits. She would complain of the monotony of their activities—all of which were interests of Sean's, pleading to undertake a new hobby or visit with friends. Sean denied all appeals, refusing to go to the theatre, even the productions that Virginia directed at school. He was only happy when they were busy with one of his hobbies. Virginia became dissatisfied with the relationship and yet balked at leaving for fear of returning to loneliness. Her passion for food resumed and she went from size 11 to 18; from trim and tan to downright overweight.

One evening in May, 1963, Sean and Virginia were having dinner at the races. During coffee both leaned back in their chairs and sat silently staring past the other with eyes seemingly glazed and unfocused. "We've got to make a decision, Sean," Virginia said without looking at him. "We should get married or break up."

"Okay," he said quietly looking from his plate to her with eyes unchanged and voice monotone. "Let's get married."

"Are you serious, Sean?" eyes focusing. "You want to marry me?" Silence.

Finally Sean said, "Would I joke about something as serious as marriage?"

"You'll have to ask my father for my hand. It's an Armenian tradition."

His face clouded and he shook his head. "No, I won't do that. I know how much he disapproves of us."

Virginia looked down at her half-eaten dinner and said, "Do what you want, Sean. I don't care."

Two weeks later he surprised her with a diamond ring, presented it in his car in front of her house. He formally asked for her hand in marriage and Virginia consented, though disappointed Hyreeg had not been asked for his blessing. She said goodnight and walked slowly into the house.

The following afternoon she approached Hyreeg, who was working in his vegetable garden.

"Sean and I are engaged, Hyreeg. See my ring?" her voice whispered and choked.

Hyreeg dropped his hoe and stared at her, looking as though someone had just driven a stake through his heart. Virginia ran with tears to her room, knowing that marriage to Sean would surely alienate her from Hyreeg and that she would likely lose his respect.

Confused and heartbroken she decided to escape her troubles by booking passage to New York City, where Margo and Saul had moved after returning from Spain. She told Sean she needed time to think a bit to ensure that marriage was the correct step. She departed for the summer leaving no forwarding address or telephone number.

In New York there was immediate comfort from the nameless faceless crowds of the city. No one could know or judge her nor interfere with her life's decisions. She could act as she pleased and answer to no one. That first day Margo and Saul met her at LaGuardia and took her to a Chinese restaurant.

"Tell me the things you like best about Sean," Margo said after ordering.

"He's generous and trustworthy. He's kind and thoughtful and likes to help other people. He's cheerful, has a good sense of humor and he's a good cook."

"Now give us the minuses."

"We don't have much in common. He's sports-minded and has no interest in cultural events or music. Prefers to be alone, not with friends. I've seen flashes of a mean streak in him and a bad temper." She reached for a napkin and rumpled it. "Sometimes I'm afraid of him."

"Has he done anything?" asked Saul. "I mean, if he has, you should get away as soon as possible. No one should put up with that."

"He hasn't been violent with me but becomes very nasty when he's angry, he shouts and swears. Nothing to me, though."

Margo drew in a sharp breath. "You have some hard facts to face, Ginny. This relationship sounds like a dead end. You're living to please him instead of yourself. That's not love, that's dependency. No wonder you're not happy."

Saul nodded and said, "It's detracting from your life, not enriching it. I would break it off right now. Return the ring—mail it to him today. You'll be much better off."

"I can't do that. I'll be alone again. I know this is a nowhere relationship; when I'm with him I don't feel as lonely, yet when I am with him, I'm not happy."

"Being alone is better than being in a miserable relationship and committed to the wrong man."

That afternoon Virginia mailed the ring back to Sean from New York without explanation. When she returned home she told her parents that the engagement was off. Hyreeg embraced her. "Vehrsheen, it's hard for you now but you have done the right thing. You will find good man someday."

The following evening Hyreeg, Myreeg and Virginia were in the living room watching *I Love Lucy* when the doorbell rang.

"I'll get it," said Virginia, running to the door. Sean was standing red-faced. She motioned for him to go out onto the porch where she joined him after closing the front door. He thrust the ring under her nose. "What the hell is this all about?" he demanded. "Who do you think you are, an Armenian Princess? I'm not good enough for you or your family? Is that it?"

"Please calm down, Sean. My parents will hear you."

Sean stalked around the porch, ranting. "You're almost thirty years old, yet you can't make your own decisions. You have to run around getting other opinions. Your father says, 'He's not good enough for you,' and you jump. Your friends say, 'You can do better,' and you jump. Don't be such a baby...grow up!"

Virginia backed up against the screen door. "It's not your fault, Sean...I'm afraid of marriage. I wasn't honest with you or myself. You've been a lifejacket for me, kept me afloat when I needed someone's attention, and I'll always be grateful. But that's not a healthy basis for marriage."

"We can go to a marriage counselor, Virginia. Give this a chance—please, I want it to work."

"Sean, I don't want to be engaged. Keep the ring. But I will go to a counselor if you will call and make the appointment."

Sean nodded and left. Virginia returned to the living room just as Lucy was getting a pie in the face. Myreeg and Hyreeg were laughing.

"Who was it, Vehrsheen?" Hyreeg asked.

"Some neighbor from across the street. Their power is out."

*   *   *   *

In the sixties a person who sought help from a counselor was assumed to be mentally ill. Virginia had reservations about subjecting herself to intimate scrutiny, yet the marriage counselor, Mr. Chadwick, was a likable man who listened attentively and with sympathy, seeing them in separate sessions.

During counseling Sean and Virginia resumed their relationship, despite drifting further apart. As Mr. Chadwick helped Sean become more independent, Virginia's insecurity increased, and thus she clung to Sean even more. After several months, however, Virginia found herself looking forward to the sessions because the insights had helped her become more self-confident.

"You know, Virginia," Mr. Chadwick said during one session. "It's not unusual for counseling to cause people to break up.   As each person becomes more emotionally stable, they become less dependent on each other."

*   *   *   *

One mid-February evening while driving home with Sean from his cousin's wedding reception the car swerved erratically on the edge of a winding elevated road.

"Sean, let me drive!" said Virginia with urgency.

"What'samatter? Don't ya' think I c'n drive?"

"You had too much to drink at the reception."

"Too much for yooou maybe. Not for me. I'll show ya' how t' drive."

He jammed down the accelerator. The car sped over the icy road, swaying over the yellow line and then back to the shoulder.

"Sean!" Virginia screamed. "You'll kill us both!"

Sean laughed and continued. Virginia slipped down on the floor under the dashboard, gripping her knees.

Twenty minutes later he screeched to a stop in front of her brother's house.

"Git outta m' car," he cried. "I don't care how th' hell ya' git home."

She glared at him for a moment, partly in anger, partly in confusion and partly in sadness. He returned the glare, then stared ahead. Virginia stepped out of the car, slammed the door and watched Sean speed away, tires squealing, swerving right and left nearly driving into a snow bank further down the block.

She made her way up to the house and rang the doorbell. Within a few minutes the porch light came on and Johnny appeared in a bathrobe, rubbing his eyes, which were still adjusting to the light. "For God's sake, Virginia. It's two a.m. What are you doing here at this hour? You okay?"

"Can I sleep here tonight, Johnny? Sean and I just split up."

"He dropped you on my doorstep?"

"I just dropped him."

Virginia's first blush of romance ended without her understanding the reasons for its angry conclusion. It was seemingly just another argument with Sean: there had been many others like it, yet the end result had never been so drastic. Myreeg and Hyreeg made no secret of their pleasure over the break-up. Things reverted back to the routine from before Sean appeared in her life; Myreeg and Hyreeg went on about their business with renewed zest instead of hassling over their dislike for the relationship, while ignorant of Virginia's growing anxiety and depression. Mr. Chadwick and her students filled the loneliness, as did music. Time away from school was spent at the piano or behind the door of Mr. Chadwick's office, or in her room alone, privately thinking of Sean. Even though she vowed never to call him again, Virginia wondered how he was and what he was doing. Was he as lonely and miserable as she? Did he ever think of her? Every effort was made to forget, but the more she tried the more his presence persisted. Week after week Mr. Chadwick listened to her reminisce of times with Sean and of the pain from breaking apart. The depression seemed to increase with each weekly visit, augmenting as the reasons for her break-up and subsequent clinging became clear. Mr. Chadwick insisted that thoughts of Sean were now a waste of energy, citing sufficient time had passed which made it reasonable to assume he'd moved on and that she needed to do the same.

Concern consequently shifted from Sean to her own physical appearance and ability to attract another man. Much to her dismay, Mr. Chadwick suggested she take a modeling course to become more in tune with the conservative style of dress and demeanor, saying her current Avant-garde apparel was too masculine for most men and a different approach would appeal to those of a more sophisticated nature. A growing preoccupation over whether or not Mr. Chadwick genuinely cared for her condition left Virginia with new worries. She realized that each week they discussed the same story, the same events, the same life, and their conversations were becoming repetitious. It seemed to her his only real motivation for listening was the knowledge he'd be getting an easy paycheck at the end of the session. Eventually, she followed his familiar advice to explore new social surroundings by taking on a graduate music class at night and another in professional modeling.

According to Mr. Chadwick, one obstacle still hindered her from letting go of the past, and attention shifted to overcoming it. "To mature emotionally you have to emancipate yourself from your parents and find independence. So long as you're living at home, this cannot happen."

Virginia felt her stomach twist. The thought of leaving home terrified her, as did the knowledge Myreeg and Hyreeg would be offended, considering it an act of betrayal. They would say all of their pleasures had been sacrificed to provide for her, to educate and assist her in any and all ways possible. She recalled how enthusiastic she'd been to move out to California, only to be persuaded to remain at home. It was socially acceptable back then to live at home, but she realized now she was too old to be living with her parents; the time had come for her to decide herself what the best course of future action should be. Mr. Chadwick coached her, emphatically saying she needed to set a deadline in order to attain her goal. She broke the news to Myreeg and Hyreeg that she would move into an apartment after the first of the year.

Both Hyreeg and Myreeg looked up from their shish ka bob and stared. Hyreeg vehemently insisted that she was fine where she was, that they provided everything for her. "Out in the world by yourself, you will only be lost. You belong with us."

Myreeg joined the argument. "There's no reason for you to pay rent when you can live with us, Vehrsheen. It's a waste of money."

In the end, with the persistence and encouragement from Mr. Chadwick, Virginia moved into an apartment located ten minutes from Myreeg and Hyreeg. The apartment was on the second floor of an old wooden building in a run-down Pontiac neighborhood; it lacked any luxury but the rent was cheap so Hyreeg and Myreeg were happy. Hyreeg was afraid the place was a fire hazard, so he brought over a thick rope on the second day and tied it to the bedpost so that Virginia could make a quick getaway out the window in case of a fire. When Virginia's baby grand piano and slate cocktail table were moved in, the living room floor sagged from the weight. Virginia's friends came over to see the apartment, and kiddingly nicknamed it "Tobacco Road" because of its seedy location and run-down appearance.

As the weeks passed and she settled into the apartment, Virginia frequently resorted to talking with Hyreeg and Myreeg over the phone or visiting them. She had her piano, her TV, her dog, but little else. Due to an increasing boredom, she joined the church choir just to have a place to go regularly. While there, she met Hilda, who was a respected psychiatrist, and the two became fast friends; Virginia drove her to choir practice on Wednesdays and used the time to confide. Hilda expressed concern for Virginia's self isolation and continuing depression.

"You can't just sit in the apartment and mope your life away, Virginia. You've got to get out among people and develop your social skills or your depressions will only worsen."

Virginia was unmoved by the arguments. Life held little happiness for her...only a persistent feeling of emptiness. Hilda continued to badger her to get out more and eventually convinced her to attend a single's dance at the YWCA. Before they entered, Virginia emphatically declared, "I'll stay for one hour, Hilda, and that's it. Don't try to make me dance with anyone."

Virginia found an empty corner and sat on a folding chair. Hilda had no trouble finding a waltz partner and trotted out onto the club floor. Virginia felt awkward by herself, but tried to concentrate on the music from the live band. The numerous faces appeared as lonely and sad as she felt. Toward the end of the hour a man approached her, asking for a dance.

"I'm sorry," she replied. "My friend and I are just about to leave. I'm a teacher and I have to get up early."

"Oh, that's too bad," he said pleasantly. Though nondescript in appearance, he had very large dark eyes and a friendly smile. "I don't have to get up until ten."

"Oh? What kind of work do you do that lets you sleep in so late?"

"I'm an interior decorator."

Virginia asked, "Are you Greek?"

"No," he replied. "Armenian."

"Pahrev," she said with growing interest. *"Inch bess es?"* (How are you?)

"Shod lave yem." (I'm fine.)

Hilda approached, wearily suggesting from her tired expression that she was ready to leave. Virginia said goodbye to the friendly Armenian gentleman, who politely walked them to their car.

"Perhaps I could see you again?" he suggested, taking her arm and helping her into the car. "Can I call you sometime?"

She nodded and hastily scrawled her number on an old newspaper.

Thus a new relationship flourished. Aram Manoogian was from France, but had lived in the United States for six years. It was his family's dream for him to come to the United States and find wealth enough to send the remaining relatives over. Originally, the intent was to have his cousin give employment and eventually make Aram a partner within his chain of shoe stores. But this dream fizzled and left Aram floundering in a strange land with very little English language speaking skills. He rented a room from his immigrant uncle, who lived in a low income area in Detroit. The uncle didn't know English and depended on Aram for interpretations. Aram floated from job to job and finally found employment with a wealthy Armenian entrepreneur, hoping to build his savings so that one day he might open his own interior decorating business.

Whenever Aram was in Virginia's company, he was always the gentleman; impeccably polite, never imposing his personal views on anyone. He was a proud man with an excellent taste for clothes, gourmet foods and special wines. He knew Armenian, French and Greek folk songs, which he sang to his guitar accompaniment. Evenings were spent sharing Armenian music or preparing gourmet Armenian dishes, or learning Armenian Art and Language. Yet all throughout, Virginia was on her guard, remaining firm in the resolve to never again entrust her feelings to a man unless she was certain he handled them with loving care.

Virginia seemed to be directing their activities together, suggesting they attend musicals, jazz concerts and visiting antique shows. Something always seemed to bother Aram as he was nearly always preoccupied. Virginia grew tired to taking on all the responsibility and when she complained to him of his lack of enthusiasm, Aram seemed genuinely apologetic and resolved to make a better effort; yet his preoccupation persisted.

After four months, she began to entertain thoughts of marriage. Again, her need to conform and be like her friends, and to live up to Hyreeg's great hopes started to gnaw away at her. For once, she saw opportunity to fit in with her peers and she knew it would make Hyreeg happy, especially if she married an Armenian. She wanted marriage only for the position of respect and stability it brought, not out of any real desire or love. She was in her middle thirties and feared by the time she was forty her chances to marry and raise a family would be slim.

Aram's unstable financial status was problematic. Virginia felt embarrassed being seen in his old car and wondered what kind of lifestyle they would have if she married him. It also bothered her she was making substantially more money than he was.

One night, after driving home from a dinner party, she broached the subject of marriage to him.

"I'm well past the age of dating just for fun, Aram. I need to know if our relationship is going to lead to anything."

"Yes, I think so, Virginia," he replied. "Let's take another two months to get to know each other better and then talk about marriage. You might say in the meantime that we're informally engaged."

Virginia sensed a hesitancy in Aram's reply but agreed, intensely eager to make the commitment endure. Her emotions skyrocketed. Anticipating a bridal veil around Easter, she broke the news to Hyreeg and Myreeg of its potential. Hyreeg was overjoyed, but Myreeg's eyes were lowered in silent thought. Her face showed no happiness. Virginia remembered how Myreeg complained when Johnny married, insisting he was too young, too poor and unemployed. Yet Johnny's marriage worked, and still Myreeg complained. She never encouraged Virginia to marry, either.   Despite this discouragement, Virginia nevertheless threw herself into the exciting relationship of dating, attending plays, concerts, and restaurants.   For a month and a half it was whirlwind of pleasant activities, and a temporary reprieve from her former loneliness and isolation.

After two months, however, a telegram arrived. Aram informed Virginia that his father would be arriving in the States in four days.

"I'm anxious to meet him," she said. Aram didn't say a word. Virginia thought the timing was perfect because she could get to know her future in-law before the wedding. Yet two weeks passed and there was no mention of marriage or of her meeting his father, and she became suspicious and upset over his secretive behavior.   Each time she broached the subject, he gave excuses that his father was too busy attending dinners given by relatives. Soon Virginia demanded to meet his father, exasperated by the delays.   He took her to his uncle's, where all his relatives met her with a cold reception.   Virginia sensed that they thought she was not appropriate for Aram. "Maybe Aram's father doesn't like American girls," she thought to herself.   After the visit, she burst out, "Aram, your father isn't friendly.   Did I say or do something wrong?"

"No.   He's been preoccupied.   His haberdashery business has gone bankrupt and he's come here to ask for my help. I will now have to support him, my mother, two sisters and my unemployed brother. I don't know how I'm going to manage with my salary, I need money."

Virginia was confused. "How will that effect us?"

"I'm afraid it means we can't marry. I couldn't ask you to get into a financial situation like mine.   Listen, Virginia. Let me explain. It hurts me terribly that events have turned out this way, but it's beyond my control. I've enjoyed your company more than anyone I've ever known...but, well, you've never been in a desperate situation with the support of your family completely hovering over your shoulders. You don't know what it's like to find yourself in a foreign country, with very little language skills and no one to back you up financially.

Besides, my father thinks I should start attending the single's club at the Armenian Church on Friday nights."

Virginia was shocked. "What are you talking about? Here I'm planning to marry you and now that your father thinks I'm not the financial rock you thought I was, he thinks you should scout around to meet a more appropriate Armenian to give you money so you can bring over the family and take care of them. What's wrong with you? Do you think I'm not wealthy enough? Is that all you're interested in?"

He shook his head and offered no explanation.

Without saying a word or looking at him, Virginia got out of the car and walked to her apartment. In the privacy of her bedroom she wept. Three days passed and there was no word from Aram. His best friend, Harold, called and gave the message that Aram had received an urgent telegram from his family in France and that he and his father had gone. Virginia never heard from him again.

Thus, evenings were once again spent alone weeping in her apartment. She vowed never again to get involved in a romantic relationship, and within a month moved back in with Myreeg and Hyreeg.

Chapter 15

Thanksgiving day, 1974, was a day of celebration for Michael and Victoria; it was the 30th anniversary of their becoming naturalized American citizens. To celebrate the event, the entire Haroutunian clan of twenty-five were invited to an enormous Thanksgiving feast. Victoria spent several days preparing katah, stuffed grape leaves, paklavah and turkey. Her arms ached from the hours of rolling out the dough for the katah.

The families arrived offering their congratulations and a small gift to mark the occasion, usually a bottle of fine Chianti. Before dinner was served, "The Lord's Prayer" was said in Armenian; heads bowed low and voices were hushed save for one young cousin mumbling impatiently, eager to indulge himself in turkey. The family feasted on Victoria's labors, helping themselves to the Armenian breads, appetizers and deserts while happily drinking. Smiles covered every face around the table as Michael's brother Armen stood offering a toast. "May God bless this country and may He bless Michael and Victoria for their goodness and perseverance. May you both live in good health for one hundred years. Congratulations on thirty years in America."

After the heavy meal the adults gathered their wine glasses and walked into the living room to sit back and talk of Armenia and all the remaining relatives. Michael mentioned that he had recently heard from his cousin Nahzar, whom he had not heard from in nearly forty years due to a ban prohibiting correspondence from anywhere outside of Armenia USSR. The ban having been recently lifted, a quick correspondence revealed Nahzar was not doing well. "His son Soorig had a bad accident," said

Michael grimly. "He's better but Nahzar afraid to leave him for long." He sighed. "I would like to see my cousin again before I die. We were very close for long time."

Virginia, thinking that travel to Armenia would help get her mind off of her depression and Aram and it would also be an educational opportunity to learn about her heritage, interrupted, "Hyreeg, why don't we go to him?"

Michael looked at her. "Go there?"

"Sure. Americans can travel in USSR now. We could go for a whole month."

"Don't be crazy." Armen's deep voice silenced everyone. "That's six thousand miles away. Politics in Russia so uncertain and dangerous. Best not to go there...you might not come back!"

"Why do you say that?" Michael asked. "I've heard talk of plenty Armenians going there and coming back safe, with no trouble. I don't think it would be problem at all." He added, as if to avoid arguing, "Don't worry, it's just an idea. I'm not really considering it—I just think it would be great to see the old relatives again."

Armen nodded and smiled, raising his wine glass. "To Nahzar and all the Haroutunians in Armenia. May we all one day be reunited!"

For several weeks after the Thanksgiving dinner, Michael and Victoria debated over whether or not to visit their homeland. Victoria was vehemently against spending the money and insisted that such travel was dangerous. Michael persisted in favor planning such a trip, arguing that Virginia ought to see the land of her ancestors, that it would show the family heritage. In the end, Victoria reluctantly agreed, weary from Michael's and Virginia's determination to visit. In the subsequent months after the New Year, papers were filed applying for passports and visas; they visited the doctor for immunization shots; I.D. photos were taken; shoes, clothes and luggage were purchased, as well as a Polaroid camera and tape recorder.

The night before departure, Armen and all the Haroutunian relatives gathered in Pontiac to say goodbye, wishing Victoria, Virginia and Michael a safe journey and giving a small sum of money and gifts for them to present to Nahzar and his family from those in Michigan. In addition the tape recorder was passed and each relative left a

detailed message to be played for the Haroutunians in
Armenia. Armen, after learning via letter from Nahzar of
the enthusiastic reaction Michael, Victoria and Virginia's
visit stirred, was quite envious of their going and insisted
that many photographs be taken and conversations
recorded for the benefit of those still in Michigan.

On the day of departure, July 20th, Johnny drove
Michael, Victoria and Virginia to Metropolitan Airport,
smiling at Michael's last-minute instructions for house-
sitting. Johnny was busy with his children and selling
used cars and could not make the trip.

The itinerary took them first to Copenhagen, where
they changed to a Soviet airliner for the flight to the Soviet
Union. When they arrived in Moscow, a clerk announced
that the plane to Armenia had been delayed four hours;
they sat on hard plastic chairs in the basement of the drab
airport; there were no windows, television, lounge or even a
restaurant, merely a small concession counter which sold
vodka and crackers. Michael bought a fifth of vodka and
several packets of crackers, giving Victoria and Virginia
each a packet and saving the vodka for himself. They
attempted to pass the time talking about what they envi-
sioned Eastern Armenia to be in the modern day.

Two young men approached and sat next to Michael,
beginning to speak in broken English.

"You American?" one asked.

Michael knew a bit of Russian. *"Da,"* he replied.

"Iss goot," they said, smiling. "Iss goot."

Michael offered the bottle of vodka to the two young
men, who were from Baku, capitol of Azerbaijan. They
happily accepted, taking turns swigging the coarse, cheap
drink and then returning it to Michael, who smiled to them
and took a drink.

"Gharahshow," (very good) said one.

"Vut state?" one of them asked Victoria.

"Michigan," she replied. "Mish-a-gun."

A stewardess came over to Michael and interrupted.
"Your plane is ready, folks. The flight is back on schedule."

Michael, Victoria and Virginia stood to leave.

"Dasbeedonyah," Michael said to the young men.

"Spaseebo." (Thank you).   They said smiling, pointing to the empty vodka bottle.

The "airliner" from Moscow to Yerevan was an old C-47 relic from World War II.   When airborne, the pilot announced, "We will be cruising at an altitude of 6500 feet. Estimated time of arrival at Yerevan, approximately 3:35 p.m.   You can unfasten your seat belts now and please enjoy the trip."

In Yerevan, the capitol of Armenia, they exited the plane and were approached by a man in a business suit. "I am Mr. Sacko with the office of Intourists," he said, shaking Michael's hand. "At your service, sir. Please follow me." He led them into a gigantic building that looked like an old abandoned post office. Michael presumed this to be the airport.

"Where will our relatives meet us?"   Michael asked while walking.

"They should have been here by now," replied Mr. Sacko. "Must be a mix-up. But I will see to it that you are taken to your assigned hotel. Perhaps they will meet you there." He led the three visitors out onto a large concourse, where he hailed a cab.

"Take these people to the Ani hotel," he instructed the driver. Turning to Michael, he apologized. "The mix-up is most unfortunate."

The cab pulled up at the Ani hotel in the center of the city. "Iss here," the cab driver said, opening the door.

"Shanorahgahlitune," Michael said, thanking him in Armenian. He reached into his pocket for a Kennedy half-dollar, given more as a collectible than compensation.

The driver's eyelids fluttered open, *"Shanorah-gahlitune,"* he said, smiling and tipping his hat.

Michael and Victoria's room was on the third floor, with Virginia next door. An Armenian woman sat behind a table in the hallway at the landing on the third floor, monitoring the hotel guests as they entered and exited the rooms. As Michael opened the door the telephone rang and he hurried to answer.

"This is Karnig, Nahzar's son. I am sorry we missed you at the airport."

Michael said, "That's all right. We got here safe. It's good to hear your voice. Where are you?"

"There was terrible confusion," he explained. "My father was misinformed about the date of your arrival, and he went to the airport a week early by mistake. Father lives in Alaverdi, a five hour drive on an unpaved road. He will come back in two or three days to see you. Will you be all right until then?"

"Yes," Michael responded. "We wanted to sightsee anyway."

Chapter 16

The following afternoon, about an hour prior to dinner, cousin Karnig arrived at the hotel to present himself to the American cousins. After an emotional introduction Karnig suggested a restaurant where other relatives of his were waiting. "Sergio, my mother's brother's son, and his wife Anna would be honored to meet you," he announced. Michael nodded and said the honor was theirs.

Karnig's resemblance to Nahzar was remarkable; It was a face that Michael recalled from long ago in a world very distant; the eyes seemed to display the same optimism Nahzar's once had as a teenager. Michael instantly liked Karnig, marveling at his seemingly positive outlook despite residing in a troubled land where living conditions had few signs of improvement. Karnig was of medium build, curly black hair and fair skin. When he smiled, a mouth full of gold fillings was noticeable. He explained that these gold fillings were a trend in Armenia; the more fillings one had, the more prosperous his family.

As they walked down the street, Karnig described various landmarks, noting the large water fountain in the middle of Lenin's Square which served as a decorative attraction. Opposite the fountain, an Armenian movie theatre displayed gigantic Armenian titles on the marquee of films which Michael and Victoria had never heard of before. Masses of people crowded the sidewalks, vendors called out for souvenirs while men played backgammon or read their newspapers in the park. Armenian music blared from lap radios of teenagers sitting around the fountain laughing; romance songs or other cheerful melodies played over the radio from the oud, clarinet and drums. The pungent odors of shish ka bob and grilled onions, peppers and tomatoes wafted down the narrow streets.

They met Sergio and Anna at the restaurant and after introductions Sergio said with a smile, "I feel like I already know all of you. Karnig never stops talking about you—the pride of America!" He laughed as he shook Michael's hand.

They all sat at a specially reserved table with an adjoining buffet of Armenian foods. Sergio began asking questions of life in America, specifically what each of them did for employment and was life as good as it was here.

"What do you do, Virginia?" he asked.

She looked up from her plate, surprised the attention was upon her instead of Hyreeg. "I teach music at a Junior High in Pontiac."

Everyone looked at her and nodded, impressed. She explained her daily schedule of classes and highlighted the musicals she'd directed, which left the listeners captivated.

Sergio said, "We have a piano at our apartment. When we return, would you do us the honor of playing something?"

"I'd be happy to. I know an Armenian song, 'Anush Kahroon.' (Sweet Spring)."

"That's my favorite song!" Anna exclaimed.

Sergio leaned over and put some bread on his plate, nodding. "That's a promise." He turned to Michael and asked, "Are the cars in America expensive? Can a working man buy one? No one here can afford a car. We walk or ride the bus or bicycle."

"The factories in America make thousands of cars every day," Michael boasted. "Cars are cheaper there. An average working man can afford to buy one. Sometimes have two or three cars for whole family."

"Ohhh my! That's amazing!" Karnig declared. "I'd give anything for a car, just one." Everyone at the table nodded their agreement.

Anna asked Victoria, "What is the shopping like in America? We have very few stores here, and there's not much to choose from. Our clothes look the same on everyone. Housedresses, that's all we wear."

"In America iss different," Victoria said. "We have lots of stores all under one roof so shoppers are not out in rain or cold weather. Some stores even stay open all night. Americans don't pay with money all the time, can pay with plastic card and the store sends bill later."

"Never heard of such a thing," Anna laughed. "You mean you just show the card, take the dress home, and pay for it later?"

"Well, you have to pay so much a month on the bill until iss paid for. The bad thing iss you can build up a terrible debt."

Michael interrupted. "We pay cash or go without. I make enough to pay our bills."

"Do you have to work?" Sergio asked Michael. "Here, after we finish school, the Government assigns us a job for life. Mostly manual labor—builders of houses and roads. Our Soviet Government looks over us like a father. We don't go hungry, but the government doesn't believe in spoiling people with fancy clothes and cars, TV sets, and big houses."

Michael frowned and shook his head. "I noticed most of the people here have three families living in a three-room apartment where some sleep on fold-out couches and the rest are left with the hard floor. You wash clothes on a wash board, there is no indoor plumbing. You have no hope of ever improving your lifestyle. Here you are working harder—to carry water and cultivate your rocky soil just to have enough to eat. You labor to live, in America we labor to live and enjoy the benefits of our work."

Sergio had been watching Michael closely. His face flushed with red for a moment as he gripped his soup spoon like a dagger. He began to speak but cut himself short after a moment and merely looked down to stir his madzoon soup.

Michael also sat quietly thinking to himself. "Life is so different now. I thought I never changed, always thought I did Armenian way, but without knowing I support American way. Always tried to keep Armenian tradition but being away so long I've become American."

After dinner they hailed a cab and drove to a park situated on top of the highest hill in Yerevan. The view overlooked the entire city, the lights from the buildings dotting the blackened landscape as a soft breeze fanned the air with the scent of cedar trees was breathtaking. This country had become the first Christian nation in 302 A.D., and the Armenian people had fought many bloody battles to protect their homes and churches.

Victoria, thinking of how little the way of life and people had changed, walked ahead of the others. Karnig and his cousins were all very outgoing and friendly; each had shown great pride for their country and its leaders and strong resistance to opposition. Their way of life was hard, but they were committed to it and they respected the work that was put in. It was a commitment which made her envious, she'd known few people in America who demonstrated such fierce backing for their lifestyle and their nation's leaders. She was very happy among these people who openly and warmly accepted her. Yet at the same time, Victoria was saddened: it was as if she was a stranger in her own homeland—she had no part in its life, its people or existence and her visit was merely superficial; people would be happy at her arrival, celebrate, and speak of it proudly to friends but when she left they'd resume their lifestyle of hard labor while she would return to comfort in America.

Walking further, Victoria came into view of the large monument *Myr Hyahstan,* Mother Armenia, a statue of a simple peasant woman towering over the city of Yerevan, a tribute to the strength and courage of all Armenian women throughout the centuries. Victoria stood at the base of the huge monument and leaned back to study the majestic woman clasping a long sword in both hands high above her. The determined look on her sturdy peasant face clearly showed she was ready to fight for her family and country.

The others caught up to Victoria and gazed at the statue. For several moments no one spoke, each lost in their own admiration for the heroic woman. Michael said, "This is almost as large as the towering Jesus in Brazil. Impressive. As big and important as the women it depicts." Everyone murmured their agreement and turned slowly to continue walking. Victoria lingered a moment until all had moved on.

*   *   *   *

Cousin Nahzar arrived at the hotel in early morning two days later. A hotel clerk had called Michael's room and announced the visitor. Barely dressed, he rushed to find his best shirt and pants while encouraging Victoria to dress likewise. He knocked on the wall and shouted for Virginia to come to their room. She appeared, moments later, standing with her parents and eagerly awaiting the imminent knock. When it came, Michael walked over quickly with hands shaking and turned the knob. Before him stood his cousin and very close friend from long ago, now an old man with most of his hair gone and slower in his step, using the aid of a cane. Behind him stood a young man.

"Nahzar, my cousin!" Michael cried, embracing him. "Over forty years have passed us. We have changed, yes?"

Nahzar held him close. "We were like brothers a long time ago. Now we must get acquainted again." He slapped Michael on the back and looked to the women who stood behind him watching the scene with broad smiles. Michael introduced his wife and daughter and Nahzar bowed deeply. "It makes me happy to see my cousin has such a lovely wife and daughter. Welcome. You are one of us." He kissed each on their forehead and then introduced the young man standing behind him in the doorway. "This is Hovig, my sister Rose's son." The young man stepped into the room and bowed.

"It is a pleasure to meet you, Hovig. I hope we see your mother as well?"

Nahzar nodded and said, "You'll meet her and my sister Agnes later."

"How is your health, Nahzar? Why do you use a cane?"

"Had a small stroke," he replied. "But iss all right now. At the time it feel like something come and take top of my head off. I lay on the ground and couldn't move until my son Yervant come and take me to doctor. This was a few years back on New Year's Eve."

After several moments of talk they all walked to the hotel restaurant, where a large breakfast had been prepared. Nahzar said, "We have forty years of stories to share. We will need big appetite, yes?"

Michael laughed and slapped him on the back, as if to say the time had not changed their loyalties. Victoria and Virginia both noted how uncharacteristically relaxed Michael was in the presence of his cousin. They laughed together at childhood pranks and exploits and shared memories of their now very different lives.

After breakfast Michael insisted that they go across the street to the American Dollar Store to buy Nahzar an apartment-size refrigerator for two hundred dollars. An Armenian citizen was not allowed to purchase items from the American store and usually had to wait years to buy an appliance. After much arguing Michael convinced Nahzar to accept his gift. They made the proper arrangements to have the refrigerator picked up later that day with a borrowed truck.

In the meantime they drove to Sergio's flat for lunch. "We go to my son Karnig's in Kirovakan after lunch. You will see more of your relatives there," Nahzar explained.

At Sergio's apartment Anna arranged the luncheon of chicken, tomatoes and cucumbers in a sandwich of lavash bread.

Victoria asked Nahzar, "Do you grow all this food on your farm?"

Nahzar nodded. "I raise chickens and lambs and butcher our animals. I also keep hives." He laughed. "I grow it, the women cook it."

After lunch Sergio pointed to an upright piano against the dining room wall. "Remember your promise, Vehrsheen, to play for us? 'Anush Kahroon,' wasn't it? Can you play it from memory?"

"Yes, I can," Vehrsheen smiled. She walked to the piano and began to play.

"I'm longing for you sweet springtime.
I wait for you sleepless nights.
From the rosebush I pick a bouquet
As a gift to give to my dearest love."

Everyone applauded. Nahzar smiled. "Did you see how she play whole thing without looking at hands?" He ran his fingers up and down in the air on an imaginary keyboard, laughing.

"She is expert musician now," Michael smiled.

Anna got up to clear the table. "I wish you were here to give my daughter piano lessons. She loves music, too."

"You have a gift for music, Vehrsheen," Sergio said. "You must play concerts in America all the time, to filled auditoriums! Whoever hears your rhapsodical music is indeed made joyful." Virginia blushed.

After the piano "recital" the men left to pick up the refrigerator, returning to a large crowd of neighbors gathered around the entrance to Sergio and Anna's apartment.

"First refrigerator in the building," Sergio explained to Michael with some embarrassment.

The men lifted the appliance from the truck and stopped several times on the walkway for admirers to look at and touch the sacred object. Curious passersby from the street noticed the commotion and walked to see. Eventually they were able to get through the crowd and managed to load the refrigerator into Anna's kitchen where it would remain temporarily until later arrangements were made to have it delivered to Nahzar's house.

After installing the refrigerator Michael and Nahzar, Victoria and Virginia departed for Kirovakan: forty five miles away, where they would spend the night at Karnig's apartment. Arriving shortly after dusk, they met Karnig's wife Heghinay and their three children who were standing in front of the building in wait.

"You're here! You're here!" Heghinay cried, hugging and kissing Victoria. "Children, come greet your aunt and uncle from America."

Her children Anahid, 10; Nuneh, 7; Artur, 6, came up shyly and extended their hands.

Heghinay led her company inside. Her best linen cloth covered the table. "Come sit down, dinner is ready."

At the head of the table Nahzar proposed a toast to his guests while eagerly juggling bowls of chicken, pilaf and salad. They feasted between retelling of stories, visiting late into the night. Victoria noticed that Michael couldn't seem to be apart from Nahzar for more than five minutes.

*　　*　　*　　*

Before they left the next morning, the children all gathered around their visitors. "Will you bring us to America one day, Uncle Michael?" Anahid asked.

He scooped her up in his arms. "The rules are very strict, but maybe someday it can happen."

Victoria patted Nuneh. "Don't give up hope, child. I never believed I'd get to America, but I did from a miracle. You pray for miracle and maybe it happen."

The five travelers climbed into the green Lada, a Russian made car that Michael and his brothers had given to Nahzar as a gift the year before, and headed down the unpaved rocky road. The morning was brisk and clear enough to notice the surrounding Googaratz Mountains lush with cedar and pine trees. Along the roadway they passed an old man, cane in hand, leading a flock of sheep. Hovig honked the horn and waved. The old man smiled and waved back.

Michael laughed. "Remember, Nahzar, the happy days when we were shepherd boys?"

He sighed, "Carefree without a worry but to get our sheep to the fields. Good thing we not know about future."

They drove two and a half hours from Kirovakan to Alaverdi, stopping at a half a dozen hamlets along the way to meet entire families of Haroutunians that Michael never knew existed. Invited into modest homes, the Americans were embraced by parents and children alike, all of whom lined up single file much like a greeting line for newlyweds to meet these newcomers.

Around noon the travelers arrived in Alaverdi, a remote village in the countryside. Nahzar's wife Anahid, their sons, daughters, grandchildren and his two sisters, Rose and Agnes, waited anxiously to greet them from outside Nahzar's small one-storey abode made mostly of stone and which overlooked more of the Googaratz Mountains.

The visitors emerged from the Lada and were introduced to Nahzar's family. Victoria reached into her travel bag for one of the many gifts she had carried from America for these new friends and relatives.

"This is for you, Anahid. I hope you like it."

Anahid ripped open the package and found a pink robe with ruffles and lace around the collar and sleeves. "Iss wonderful, Victoria. Thank you!" she said, displaying the robe proudly for all to see.

Michael grinned. "We have something for everyone, Nahzar. Perhaps Hyganoosh can distribute them."

Hyganoosh, Nahzar's eldest daughter, a robust woman of fifty, smiled and hugged Michael. "I will pass these wonderful gifts around fairly, Uncle," she promised.

"We must have a toast!" beckoned Nahzar from the kitchen as he reached for an earthenware jug on a shelf next to the front door. Anahid got some small clear glasses from another shelf and Nahzar filled them with raki, a ninety proof alcoholic drink made from boysenberries. "Iss raki I make myself," he said proudly.

Michael took one swallow and nearly dropped the glass. "Wow!" he exclaimed and fanned his mouth. "That's real firewater. Guaranteed to kill all germs for sure. Maybe us too."

"He also makes his own wine," Anahid declared. "Iss strong enough to grow hair on a bald head."

Nahzar sat back proudly with arms folded as everyone saluted his unique abilities. After a moment he stood with his glass raised and expression serious. "*Pahree agar,* (welcome) to our cousins from America and may God bless them all, may they all live in good health for a hundred years!"

"*Pahree agar!*" the others chanted in unison. "*Pahree agar!*"

Chapter 17

An hour later the children were put to bed and the adults remained seated around the kitchen table, all drinking raki, except Victoria who declined the stiff beverage after one mouthful.

The kitchen had no stove, sink, or running water, and one dim electric light bulb dangled from the middle of the ceiling. There was no telephone or heating system and cooking was done on a homemade grill in the backyard. Water from a nearby well had to be carried into the house from wooden buckets. There was no bathroom or even an outhouse, one simply squatted in a corner of the yard. These primitive conditions did not bother Michael or Victoria—it was a childhood memory, but for Virginia it was embarrassing.

"When you return home, Michael," said Nahzar while pouring himself another drink, "I want you to kiss Armen and Louis and every Haroutunian on their forehead for me."

"Better yet, come back and do it yourself, Nahzar."

"I wish I could," he said sadly. "I would go to see my cousins Armen and Louis, just once, even if I knew it would take my last breath." He sighed. "But—iss hard for me to walk now. I can't do it."

"Armen and Louis will understand. All the same they miss you."

Nahzar took another drink of the raki and leaned back against the chair. "Do you ever think about the time we escaped from Western Armenia, Michael?"

"I still have nightmares," Michael answered distantly, drinking from his glass twice. "Yes, I still remember. I've tried to forget but it always comes back."

He paused long enough to look over at Virginia, whose expression revealed cautious curiosity, like one wanting to open Pandora's box but not certain of what she would find. "Victoria and Vehrsheen never heard that story—" He drank again, emptying the glass. He looked at Victoria as he spoke. "It was a dark night in May when we slipped through the bands of Turkish soldiers out to kill us. They had just killed Nahzar's father, Eskandar and they wanted us dead too. Those bastards were afraid of the Haroutunians." He looked down at his glass and smiled, though his face was tight and his body rigid. "Nahzar's father killed Turks, many Turks, and they were afraid. The only way they ever caught him was through the betrayal of his best friend, Mamili, who told the Turks his every move. When they killed Eskandar, they came looking for us because they rightly knew we'd be out for blood. We narrowly escaped by crawling on our bellies for two days to get to the river, which on the other side was Dersom where citizens gave safe haven to refugees. We could barely see each other in the dark—" Michael stopped and Nahzar continued.

"That last night when we reach the river, five or six soldiers see me and start shooting so I dive into the water. That's the last time I see you, Michael. I hear lots of shooting and screaming. For years I thought they kill you that night. Until I hear from Armen ten years later that you are alive."

Nahzar grew silent.

Michael's face was grim. "The soldiers don't see me hiding in the bushes. I am scared they kill you—so much shooting at once. But when the guns stop, I hear the water splashing and soldiers cursing because you got away. I say a prayer of thanks."

"Hyreeg, I had no idea," Virginia gasped.

"That is why you cry out in your sleep?" Victoria asked quietly.

Michael nodded. "The savage dog of fear never goes away. Always inside my head."

The room was silent for many minutes. Nahzar finally jumped to his feet with glass raised. "We must drink to life. We outfoxed the Turkish bastards and we survived. Entire armies couldn't destroy our family. The

Haroutunians endured the wrath of the Turks and we will endure all other obstacles. May the name Haroutunian live on forever." Everyone raised a glass and echoed, "May the Haroutunian name live on forever."

The women of Nahzar's family scurried about preparing a special dinner in honor of the visitors, the Madagh. Part of the lamb meat would be boiled, the other part barbecued for shish ka bob.

"Iss customary here for men to eat first," Nahzar explained. "But Victoria and Vehrsheen are guests of special honor and will sit with the men."

Prayers were solemnly said and the food was eaten in near silence. Even the children and grandchildren seemed to realize the intensity from the silence and though not understanding, did not dare misbehave. When it was over, Michael and his family said goodbye to the others, as it was time to return to Yerevan and begin the long journey home. Nahzar waited until his family said their farewells in the house and then walked alone with Michael, Victoria and Vehrsheen outside. He approached Victoria first with a wide smile. Here is a ring for you, since I was not able to be at your wedding. Even though we two not known each other very long you will always have a special place in our hearts because you are the wife of Michael. He is no ordinary man, and it takes an extraordinary woman to make him happy. May God always bless you!" He placed the ring on her finger. "When you wear this, think of all of us here who love you."

Victoria embraced him. It was hard for her to speak. She looked at these people, all of whom cared for her. She looked down at the ring, which had shown such caring, and feelings welled up inside her that she did not know how to say. She just softly said, "Thank you."

Nahzar nodded and turned to Michael.

"It breaks my heart to leave you, Nahzar," Michael said, embracing him. "I am happy we had chance for reunion after all these years. Ten days together is better than none.

Nahzar held his cousin for a long moment, letting the tears fall freely as Victoria and Virginia looked on. "Do not forget me, my brother. Take care of yourself and your family. When you get home, remember to kiss every

Haroutunian on the forehead for me, especially Armen and Louis."

Michael drew away and nodded, clapping him on both shoulders. "I will brother. Stay well." He turned and ushered his wife and daughter into the waiting taxi. He got into the car, closed the door and waved one last time to Nahzar as the taxi pulled away.

Chapter 18

One morning in December, 1978, Victoria spat blood while brushing her teeth. "Vehrsheen, come look at this," she called from the bathroom.

Virginia saw the blood and immediately called the family physician, who insisted that Victoria be brought in for x-rays. After a careful examination he diagnosed bronchitis and prescribed a suitable medication.

Virginia arranged to obtain the medication and administered it to Myreeg. For several days normality seemed to resume, Victoria no longer coughed nor showed any sign of sickness. A week after starting the medication, however, Michael took Virginia aside after dinner. "Victoria keeps spitting blood. The doctor said it would stop shortly after taking the medication, but it's been over a week since she started with the medicine."

"She is? Why didn't Myreeg say anything about this?"

Michael shook his head. "She didn't tell me. I just saw her spitting a little while ago."

Virginia went to Myreeg's room, where Victoria sat reading a newspaper. "Is it true you are still spitting blood?"

Myreeg looked to her with an expression of annoyance. "Iss nothing, will go away in a few days. Leave me alone."

Virginia called an otolaryngologist whom a friend recommended. They arranged for Victoria to come in for an examination that afternoon. After running some tests, the doctor said, "In my opinion she's displaying the beginning signs of heart failure."

Virginia frowned. "She's never had heart problems."

The doctor lowered his head, peered over his glasses and raised an eyebrow, as if angry that Virginia should question his judgment. "She has now. After all, she is in her seventies."

Put off by the doctor's condescending attitude Virginia took Myreeg to yet another doctor who took more x-rays and diagnosed an enlarged heart. He spoke very academically and confidently, but Virginia was skeptical. From three doctors came three very different opinions. She took Myreeg to a fourth, who said, "We must do exploratory surgery tomorrow."

"I'll let you know," Virginia said, exasperated. She was upset and concerned for Myreeg but didn't want to hurry any treatment for fear of it being incorrect, especially since no one agreed over the diagnosis. Recalling the help she received for her own throat problems, she decided to take Myreeg to the University of Michigan Hospital where the Assistant Head of Otolaryngology listened closely to the symptoms and said, "Nine chances out of ten it isn't cancer because she's never smoked. But I do recommend a throat biopsy just to be sure."

Victoria was admitted the following day for a complete examination with Virginia close at her side. "I know you're worried, Myreeg, but I'm sure it's nothing to be concerned about. We just want to be sure you are all right, for our own piece of mind as well as yours. I'm positive you'll be home tomorrow cooking shish ka bob."

"I hope you're right, Vehrsheen." She sat twirling her thumbs. "I pray to God it's nothing serious."

Virginia wanted to take her mother's hand and comfort her, but hesitated. It was not Myreeg's way to show affection openly, nor was it hers. She just sat on the hospital bed in silence.

The biopsy was done on February 10th. Michael and Virginia were present when a team of doctors revealed the results. The head doctor looked at Victoria and said matter-of-factly, "The biopsy was positive, Mrs. Haroutunian. We've done the test twice to be certain. You have a small cancerous tumor on the lining of your trachea. That's your windpipe. It's a fast spreading type of malignant cell, which means you'll have to undergo exten-sive radiation treatments immediately."

Virginia was stunned; the word cancer to her was synonymous with death. She sat silently beside Myreeg trying to mask her own fears.

Victoria didn't move nor did she ask questions, instead simply stared straight ahead with back rigid and thumbs twirling.

"What are her chances?" Virginia asked quietly, trying to stay under control.

"Not very good, I'm afraid. As I said, this type of cell spreads rapidly. The trachea is difficult to get at with radiation. The success rate is only twenty-five percent."

"If the radiation works then she'll be cured?" Virginia pressed.

"We can't give you any guarantees. It could be terminal, it may not." He turned back to Victoria. "We will do all we can for you, Mrs. Haroutunian, but you need to fight harder than anything to help us destroy this cancer."

*   *   *   *

On a bitterly cold February morning Victoria was transferred to the University of Michigan's Cancer Clinic. Virginia was close at her side, committed to aiding Myreeg by fluffing pillows, bringing special egg lemon soup and telling cheerful stories. "Don't worry," she would say. "Everything will be all right. You have the best doctors in the world and both Hyreeg and I will be here every day to check on you."

Victoria protested. "You don't have to come every day, Vehrsheen, it's too long a drive."

"We will be here!" Virginia repeated before leaving.

The radiation treatment lasted eight weeks, leaving Victoria unable to speak and barely able to swallow; at night when the effects of the radiation set in she was in constant pain. There was a burning sensation from her chest area up to her throat, especially around her wind-pipe. The pain was so intense for her that she could not sleep, instead, she rolled and convulsed in her bed all night.

Virginia and Michael sat by her bed evenings talking about the weather, the neighbors, relatives in Armenia, Virginia's students, and whatever else came to mind that was uplifting. Myreeg would listen passively, nodding only on occasion, and never showing signs of gratitude, but never complaining. Virginia grew frustrated that Myreeg never showed emotion; she wanted to comfort her but had no idea how since Myreeg refused to reveal any of her insecurities.

As the treatment resumed and Myreeg's discomfort increased, Virginia took on the role of intermediary between her mother and the doctors and nurses, relaying any problems which Victoria would communicate only to her; she soon realized that Myreeg was hiding her physical pain from the doctors and nurses. One evening while visiting, Virginia learned Myreeg had been constipated for several days but hadn't told anyone. Virginia suspected it was out of shyness, as she had a habit of covering things from strangers. Appalled, she ran to a nurse who performed an enema at once. The constipation, however, was so bad that other methods had to be employed which were very painful. When the nurses were finished, they left Myreeg with Virginia, who sternly reproached her. "From now on don't hide things from people. If you had told the nurses of your constipation earlier, none of this would have happened. You went through all that pain just because you were too shy to tell anyone. A lot of people are in pain. That's why we have doctors, they are here to cure you. They can't do anything for you if you don't tell what's wrong." Virginia's voice was raising to a shout. "You hid your spitting of the blood and you very well could have died from that had you hid it any longer. You might have died had you hid your constipation longer. I drive fifty miles everyday to see you and you aren't making any effort to get better. People are trying to help you and you don't cooperate, you just sit and pretend nothing's wrong. Things don't just go away by ignoring them, Myreeg. You've got to make the effort to resolve them. No one knows how you are feeling, or the pain you are in, that's why you must tell the doctors, so they can make you better."

Myreeg sat in bed, looking at her feet and twirling her thumbs, resembling a small child who had just been punished and was feeling very remorseful. Virginia stood, red-faced, waiting for her to say something.

*   *   *   *

The house was empty without Myreeg's constant prodding to cook or wash or clean. Virginia keenly felt the absence and realized that she missed the constant criticisms and complaints. Over the next two months, it left her time to reflect; for the first time she began to see her Myreeg as a figure of strength, the backbone of the family—the stage manager who worked silently behind the scenes setting up props and issuing instructions to ensure that everything ran smoothly. Every night after returning from the hospital Virginia cried and prayed for her mother's health, and for the chance to show how much Myreeg meant to her.

After eight weeks of radiation, Victoria was moved to the old University of Michigan Hospital, the first university owned hospital in the country, built in 1920. The sixteen to twenty bed wards in each wing of the building were long and narrow, each bed filled with a patient.

Virginia encouraged Victoria to walk around the hospital when her strength returned, saying exercise would be good. She held Myreeg's arm in hers, walking slowly but steadily through the hallways and wards, eventually both learning every part of the third floor. When Victoria was strong enough to walk on her own, she went to the hospital chapel, located down the hall from her bed, and spent several hours daily behind the altar, pleading for her carcinoma to be cured.

Two and a half months after Victoria's admittance, a doctor came into her room while Virginia and Michael were visiting. "I have a good report," he announced with a wide smile covering his freckled face. "The cancer had gone into remission."

"That's wonderful news," cried Virginia. "Does that mean she's cured?"

"It's still too early to say," he replied. "But quite frankly, we are amazed at how well she's responded."

Michael jumped up and shook the doctor's hand. "Thank you, Doctor, thank you. You are most kind."

"Victoria is my best patient," he nodded.

With tears in her eyes Victoria reached for his hand and kissed it. "You saved my life, Doctor. God bless you."

The doctor patted her hand and smiled before motioning for Virginia to follow him into the hall. "There is no guarantee that your mother's cancer will stay in remission," he said, once out of earshot. "Make plans to take her on a trip to do whatever she would like because her time might be limited. Be sure to bring her back once a month for follow-up examinations." He smiled and added, "Enjoy your time together."

For Virginia death had never been a reality and yet the threat of her mother's life had changed all priorities. Material values lost their meaning; fretting over petty complaints was a waste of time, and socializing lost all importance. She remembered as a child how Myreeg nagged that she'd never helped around the house, that her own interests had taken priority over the interests of the family. A new energy and determination came to Virginia; pleasing Myreeg was for her, now, the primary focus. The thought of being without her was too painful to contemplate.

A few days after they arrived home Virginia announced, "Myreeg, you need a vacation. I will take you anywhere you'd like to go. How about a nice warm climate like southern California? You've never been there."

"No, no, not California!" Victoria protested. "I want to go to Ellis Island."

"Ellis Island? Why do you want to go to that old place? At least in California you can bask in the warm sunshine."

"Ellis Island. Take me to Ellis Island. Iss important."

Chapter 19

Virginia could hardly wait to begin the trip to New York. It was a chance to make good on her resolve to devote more attention to Myreeg and to show what an important influence she had been on her. The two women made the drive alone; Michael remained in Pontiac to look after the house.

"You drive carefully, Vehrsheen" he said to her, placing a basket of sandwiches and fruit in the back seat. "Call me as soon as you get there."

They left at 4:30 a.m. on a warm June morning, driving Virginia's new Catalina. They took the Canadian route, stopping in Chatham, Ontario, for breakfast, and in Niagara Falls for lunch, before driving across the dull New York Thruway for the remainder of the afternoon. Victoria was virtually silent, except to give an occasional driving instruction. Virginia was eager to know Myreeg's thoughts, but kept respectfully quiet, knowing that there was plenty of time to talk later. Her own thoughts drifted to an ever-present curiosity of why Myreeg was so eager to see Ellis Island. What happened there which prompted her to visit? Virginia knew Myreeg was an immigrant, but thought she'd come through Boston as Hyreeg had. Questions formed in her head of Myreeg's past; Ellis Island must have some personal relevance to her, as Myreeg was not one to engage in superfluous activities. Virginia recognized, as she often had before, that she knew very little of Myreeg's life; she had questioned her only on rare occasions about the past, but at each attempt Myreeg would silence her, angrily saying, "Don't ask, I don't want to talk about it." And thus Virginia eventually gave up.   She believed that since

Myreeg never spoke of the past, it was not relevant to anything and she no longer bothered to inquire of it.

The sun was setting upon reaching Hackensack, New Jersey, where they decided to spend the night.

"We'll get a good night's sleep," Virginia said as they pulled into a motel parking lot. "You'll be well-rested for Ellis Island tomorrow."

The next morning at 6:00 a.m. they left for Battery Park, stopping briefly for breakfast on the way, and arriving by 8:00 a.m. to board the first ferry for the island, where only a handful of other tourists joined for the excursion. Millions of immigrants who had helped build America had ridden a similar ferry to Ellis Island.

The Ferry House was at the end of a slip that ran through the center of the island. A young man dressed in a black uniform and brimmed hat waited under the canopy.

"Ladies and gentlemen," he called as the visitors debarked. "Welcome to Ellis Island. My name is Tom, I'll be your guide for today. Please follow me...I will first take you to the Baggage Area where incoming immigrants went to gather their luggage, which had been taken upon boarding for passage to America."

Virginia and Myreeg walked at the front of the group; eventually Myreeg was walking two paces ahead of the tour guide into the main building. As they neared the Baggage Area Victoria slowed to allow the guide to lead the group into the large open area. Tom said, "This is where the immigrants came to pick up their luggage. Some of the immigrants tried to conceal their deformities by hiding behind suitcases or parcels, but that usually didn't work because all immigrants were made to leave their belongings on the floor and climb the stairs to the Great Hall while the officials watched. If shortness of breath, lameness, or other deformity was suspected in any of the immigrants, an examiner would mark their lapel with a piece of chalk, which meant they needed a careful examination. If they failed the examination, they were rejected."

"What happened to them if they were rejected?" Virginia asked.

"They were deported, usually sent back to their homeland. It was very sad. Entire families would scrape together their last pennies for the voyage to America, only to be turned away because of some physical ailment. Sometimes one child wouldn't pass inspection and had to be separated from their family, sent back alone to their country...This tour will be confined only to the first floor of the main building, because the second and third floors are deteriorated," he laughed politely. "Parts of the walls have collapsed up on the second and third floors. Moving on...the epicenter of the main building was the Great Hall or Registry Room, where immigrants were processed. The sixty-foot high domed ceiling, constructed in 1916, is made of buff terra-cotta tiles; there are three chandeliers and several expensive half-moon windows which help to light the area. The Guastavino brothers, a Spanish immigrant family from Barcelona, designed this great dome. Within the Hall, benches were set up where immigrants sat to wait for their names to be called, each hoping to be allowed into America. The theater was located on the second floor where once a week outside performers came to entertain with stage production or variety shows. Lining the balcony of the Great Hall were fourteen dormitory rooms. In 1908 one dormitory room contained thirty-six canvas bunks in triple tiers. The library, located on the third floor near the gallery and dormitories, subscribed to nearly every international newspaper so that immigrants could follow the current events in their homeland. One can look down below to the first floor from the balconies of the second and third floors." He paused as the visitors looked up the stairway leading to the Great Hall. "It is said that 100 million or so living Americans can trace their roots to Ellis Island." He paused as the crowd let out a collective gasp of awe.

"Do any of you have friends or relatives who came through here?" he asked.

Victoria put her hand up level to her face and then down again, repeating it three times. Tom couldn't see her timid response from over the crowd so an elderly gentleman beside her called our, "Over here. This lady wants to say something."

Tom looked over and smiled. "Good. Would you come to the front please ma'am and share your experience?"

Virginia watched in surprise and awe as Myreeg stepped to the front, holding her hands together at her lap and standing like a little girl in front of a classroom. She looked timid and yet filled with the enthusiasm which comes with the recognition that she had something important to share.

"I come through Ellis Island long time ago," she began. "I stay for two and a half months in that first room by the stairs." She pointed to the room on the third floor which now looked like an ancient ruin. The plaster had crumbled away into a dirty pile on the floor already covered with rubble and dust from neglect. There was a gaping hole which left one wall barely standing, leaving only a partial configuration to give an idea of the setup. "Fifty years ago that room was new, shiny and clean...had four beds and toilet. Every night they lock our door. They clean our rooms after we leave for breakfast: we eat on this main floor in that right-hand corner." She pointed again, walking toward the area she described. "Behind these walls is the cafeteria. After the meal they take us to the recreational area outside where we exercise; none of us have coats, and it is middle of winter. Snows often and very cold, but we run to keep warm. When we finish exercise they give us crafts. I got dresser cover with rose design to embroider. I never embroider before but I learn quickly. They give us red, green, and yellow silk threads for flowers and leaves. I still have that dresser cover." All throughout, Virginia listened, captivated, still reeling from the surprise that these were her mother's experiences and that her mother was sharing them with strangers.

Victoria continued. "I never eat hot dog till I come to Ellis Island. I saw one man eat whole banana, skin and all because he never seen one where he come from. Lot to learn about in new country."

No one spoke. Myreeg had brought Ellis Island alive again with her memories and flashbacks and the tourists were all envisioning it through her words.

Tom broke the silence. "Thank you for that wonderful insight." He turned to the visitors. "Ladies and gentlemen, if you'll follow me we'll move on..."

Chapter 20

Virginia walked to a bench below Victoria's old room in the main building. The tour had just ended and they had thirty minutes before the next ferry arrived. "Let's sit here and rest a bit, Myreeg."

Victoria nodded. "I talk too much. Now my throat feel dry." Virginia handed her a water bottle which she carried since the radiation treatments. Myreeg sipped it carefully, taking short, hesitant mouthfuls. The pain from swallowing was still obvious. She sat in silence for several moments staring out, her breathing raspy and dry. She put her hand on Virginia's knee and said softly, "I carry such pain inside me, Vehrsheen. All my life I had nobody."

"What are you talking about? You have a family."

Myreeg didn't answer, so Virginia took the initiative. "What were your mother and father like?"

Victoria sat back on the bench. "I don't remember my father, Melkon. He pass away when I am six, I don't know from what. My mother, Anna, I remember had light skin and long light brown hair. She wore it pulled back and tied in a bun. She was very tall woman. I don't see my brother Manoug too much, he iss older and always out taking care of our animals in the fields. The last time I see him iss the time we crossed the Euphrates river. My baby sister Zarman—"

"You have a baby sister?" Virginia interrupted with credulity.

"Eye-yo. (Yes). I was six years older than her. Zarman had blond curly hair and a round pretty face. I wish you saw her, she was beautiful. One day she had accident. Iss my fault. My mother leave Zarman alone with me so she could get water from a nearby stream. I leave Zarman inside and go out to play. Zarman fall on our grill and burn her face. Lucky my mother hurry back just in time...Zarman don't burn her face too much.

"She take care of Zarman's burn and come to take me inside. She show me the burn on my sister's face, and said it hurt her. I was too young to realize how much it hurt, but years later when I burn my hand frying perch, I feel the pain Zarman must have felt. I feel the blame now."

She was silent. A voice echoes through the empty hallway. She spoke again.

"My real name iss Tourvanda Ahigian."

"Your name isn't Victoria?"

"After I come to this country some of my Armenian lady friends convince me to change my name to sound more American, so when I married I take the name Victoria. I don't even know my real birthday, so when people ask, I used to give a different date each time. When I come to America I ask my Cousin Dick how old I am. He told me I was a baby in 1910 when he left for America. That's how I guess my age. I choose Valentine's Day, February 14, 1908, for my birthday because iss easy to remember." She smiled at this recollection.

"We live in farming village called Palanga, south of Black Sea. My father Melkon was born there and my mother Anna was from a cultural town of Pingan situated on the banks of the Euphrates River in Western Armenia."

"How did your parents meet if they lived in different villages?" Virginia asked.

"They have no dating over there. Parents are matchmakers. When I come to live with cousins Dick and Harry, Cousin Dick tell me about my parent's wedding and how it happen. My father rode two hours on horseback to Pingan to claim his bride. After the wedding, they ride back together to Palanga, where all the Ahigian relatives began calling my mother 'Pingansee,' because she's from Pingan, and people from there regarded with great respect."

"Grandmother didn't know her husband before her wedding day?"

"That is the way in the old country," she responded matter-of-factly. "But I talk too much again, Vehrsheen, my throat is dry." She started to get to her feet. Virginia remembered how often she'd heard Myreeg say, "Love is not important. Dating is a waste of time."

"No, no, Myreeg. Please sit down and tell me more."

"My story iss sad. What happen in my life I am not proud to tell. It make me feel like I'm nothing." She stared at a spider crawling slowly over the floor. Her arms were in her lap and her face was expressionless.

"But, Myreeg, the story of your life is important. It's very important to me. I've never heard you talk about your past before and I want to know about it. Talking about it might be good for you, make you feel better." She put her hand on Myreeg's shoulder. "I want to learn more about you."

Myreeg thought for a moment. "It iss a sad story, but in Ellis Island there are many sad stories. Are you sure you want to hear mine?"

"Oh yes, yes, Myreeg. Tell me everything, where you lived, what kind of house you lived in? Who lived with you? Who did you play with?"

Victoria took in a deep breath and looked around her, as if to make sure no one was listening.

"I was born in Palanga, Western Armenia, which is Turkish Armenia today. My house is made with mud bricks. Our roof is flat but hard as cement, also made from mud. In the wintertime we use a shovel to clean snow off so roof don't cave in. The front door open to dark hallway that go to kitchen.

"My mother cook on a *mangal*, a small grill, and use wood and dung to burn. The dung is cheaper, but don't last long. There iss a place to store grain and a big clay kettle to keep water. My mother carry water from the stream in a large clay jug. In winter she sometime slip on ice and the jug break. She make my favorite food, havla, and something similar to our French toast with eggs and butter.

"You walk up two steps from our kitchen to get to a large room where we eat and sleep. We put our mattresses on the floor at night and in the morning we fold and store them on a big shelf in the wall. We get light from one long narrow window up high near ceiling. At night we burn candles that my mother make. We heat our house by moving the *mangal* full of red hot embers to a hole in the middle of the floor in the big room. We put a table over that and then a comforter, and sit on cushions with our feet under the quilt to keep warm. During the day I play hide-and-seek under the *mangal* with cousin Norah and my girlfriend Kaleesta. Of course the embers are out then.

"We eat out of one big pot placed on a low stool in the middle of the room. We sit on the floor cross-legged, each of us dipping in a long wooden spoon. In back of kitchen iss stable. We have horse, sheep, goat and chickens. My favorite animal was our reddish-brown goat named *Herishdag*, meaning Angel. Outside there iss no sidewalk, no road, no grass. Just mud. Everywhere you look, there is mud. We call our life *penahgan*, Vehrsheen. That mean natural. Nothing artificial. All our food come from our own efforts. Back then people work very hard, today things much easier."

She leaned forward with a distant look in her eyes, gazing out at the empty baggage area. "Yah, Vehrsheen, when I look back I realize how hard my mother worked. We didn't have much, but we are happy. Our relatives live close by and our house is filled with children. My mother Anna sing songs and tell stories of Armenia passed down from her mother."

Victoria's voice changed from subdued melancholy to stern reproach. "But our life turn upside-down. Trouble come. Talk of war."

"What war?"

"Young Armenian men were being drafted into Turkish army. Thousands of them escape the country to avoid draft. But my cousins and I just children and we know nothing about the trouble. We sing songs and play. Cousin Norah talk about her brothers Dick and Harry who live in America. She says 'Maybe I'll go to America one day and live with my brothers.'"

Victoria paused, looking straight ahead, lost in her thoughts. She shook her head and moaned.

"Are you getting tired, Myreeg?"

Victoria had a pensive look in her eyes. "No, Vehrsheen. I feel fine. I was just thinking how happy I am to see Ellis Island again and the Statue. I love New York because it's cooler than countries from where I come with very hot climates. I feel good whenever I'm here," she paused, "though I feel guilty sometimes that I make it here and many others do not. I'm glad we make this trip, Vehrsheen. I feel very good. Can we see the Statue of Liberty now?"

"That's a good idea," Virginia said. "We'll go as soon as the ferry pulls in." She stood and assisted Myreeg, who did not resist the touch. They walked to the dock where the ferry was loading, and joined the other passengers. Virginia led Myreeg to a bench along the railing separating boat from water where they sat together saying nothing. Virginia stared into the sparkling azure water lost in the names of her mother's relatives and of places unknown to her.

Chapter 21

Victoria and Virginia had lunch at a nearby concession stand before boarding another ferry to get to the Statue of Liberty. They sat eating hot dogs on a bench looking out at the water.

"How did you feel, Myreeg, the first time you saw the Statue?"

"Hard to believe it was fifty years ago, Vehrsheen. It feel just like a dream to me now. I look up at her and wonder if America has place for me. I talk to the Lady in my head and she say, 'Be patient. You will belong.' That give me hope."

Virginia nodded. "It must have taken courage, Myreeg, to come here alone. I couldn't have done it."

"When I look back, I wonder how I did it."

"Did you get what you were hoping for?"

"No. My life no change that much. Still poor. Still lonely. But I lost my fear in America."

They finished eating and boarded the ferry taking them to the Statue, both sitting in silence for the duration of the ride. Upon arrival they took an elevator up inside the Statue to the overlook. At a souvenir stand they bought a deck of playing cards, some postcards and a miniature replica of the Statue before sitting on benches overlooking a view of Manhattan.

"Your father will like these," Victoria said, smiling at the postcards. He never see the Statue of Liberty. Remember, he come to America through Boston." Victoria kept looking at the Torch of Liberty on her model. She slumped against the back of the bench with hands clasped and eyes closed, silent for several minutes. Finally, "I tell you now what happened to me...In 1915 Western Armenia was ruled by the Ottoman Turks. I was seven. The Turks sent a town crier to our village with a message ordering the people to be ready to leave the next morning. They could take nothing with them.

"I am excited because I'm a kid, I think we are taking a trip. But after the man left, I see Myreeg is scared. She start to cry. She say, 'They are forcing us to leave our house, our land and don't tell us where we are going.'

"Now I scared from seeing Myreeg scared and we all can't sleep that night. Next morning is bright and sunny July day. We line up in front of our house, my mother, brother, baby sister and me. Little while later my cousin Norah, Aunt Helen and other Ahigian relatives line up behind us. I notice cousin Mergiditch is not there. The neighbors line up behind us on the dirt path. One elderly neighbor, Yervant, holler, 'We gonna come back maybe next week. Don't worry.'

"Two Turkish soldiers approach with guns and whips. One holler, 'Line up! Over there in the road. No talk—no questions. Do what I say!' The other start cracking his whip on the ground to make people move faster. Yervant yell, 'Where you taking us?'

"A Turk silence him with lash of the whip and Yervant fell to the ground holding his bleeding head. Everyone afraid to help him now.

"I wrap my arms around Myreeg and feel her body tremble. She is carrying Zarman and clutching my hand. 'Never let go of my hand or you get lost,' she tell me. My older brother Manoug is right behind us as is cousin Norah, Aunt Helen and rest of my family.

"Around noon we start to walk. A Turkish soldier take our animals away and I look at my reddish-brown goat a long time, I feel he notice we not coming back. A Turkish soldier riding horseback beside us yell, 'Yuru! Yuru! Gavurs!' That means, 'Walk! Walk! Damned infidels!' So we follow like sheep."

Virginia leaned back against the park bench. Victoria's eyes were distant and her thumbs were twirling. She sat straight up and her voice broke. "The Turks make us leave the path and walk in the fields under the hot sun and we are sweating and hungry. As we walk, more and more people join us from other villages. By late afternoon we stop outside a town for the night. They don't let us have food or water. We sleep on the damp, cold ground, can't see our cousins and we are afraid to look around for them. I lay on one side of Myreeg with Zarman between us, my brother is on other side. Our eyes stay wide open all night. How can we sleep?

"I pull away and get to my knees to see if I can find Norah. I hear a sound like running and then a shout. Suddenly, a Turk with a knife jump on top of me. He look close at my face, hisses and run off, I think he going to kill me. I lay there shaking so scared but I can't scream.

"Later Myreeg whisper to an old man lying next to us, 'Do you know where Mergiditch is?'

"He put his finger to his mouth. 'Shhhh. Don't let soldiers hear us,' he whisper back. 'Mergiditch related to you?'

"'Yes. You've seen him?'

"'It don't look good for him. The Turks take all young men and strong boys and march them off to jail. It don't look good. I don't believe they are going to jail. The Turks lie—they lie about changing our place to live, so why would they tell the truth about taking the men to jail? We won't be going back to our village,' he sighed and turned over to fall asleep.

"The next morning the Turks holler, 'Walk! Walk! Gavurs!' I hear the sound of bullets and I think they are not just moving us to a different village, I think they are going to kill us all. We can't find any of our relatives and the Turks don't let us wait. To this day I don't know what happened to them."

Virginia looked to Victoria and whispered, "I've read about the Armenian Genocide of 1915, of the starvation marches. I remember hearing fragmented references at family gatherings, but I never thought you were involved in it. Stories I read in books of Turkish soldiers lining up Armenian boys in a row and riding past them on horseback, swinging their sabers and seeing who could decapitate the most; of Armenian maidens being forced to dance naked in a circle of Turkish soldiers who shot at their feet, then violated them and set them afire with kerosene. All of that doesn't seem real to me. It happened long ago in a land I hardly know and yet my family is so closely connected to it. I never knew this, Myreeg, I wish I had. It reveals a great deal about you, things I never knew that I wish I had."

Myreeg nodded and said, "I need some water. Since radiation iss hard to talk much."

Virginia handed her the water bottle and waited for her to continue.

"My Myreeg carry Zarman. Tears stream down Myreeg's face as she hold my hand and we walk. Same thing every day. We walk under sun without food or water. When we find a tiny brook we take a drink or eat berries or root plants along the way.

"We walk zigzag in the fields, I don't know why, but I guess we walk maybe twenty-five miles in three days before we reach the Euphrates River where they put my mother, brother, sister and me and many others on a raft made from inflated goat skins covered with long wooden boards. In about ten or fifteen minutes we reach other side. The Turks holler at us to keep on walking. People start to lie in road and don't get up.

"Two days after we cross the river, my mother was so weak she let go of my hand. I am numb, don't feel nothing. I am too weak from diarrhea, and I need water. I try to look for my mother, but I'm so weak iss hard for me to even walk. So many people struggling past me, some falling down and not getting up, others shoving me out of the way. I try to look at the faces, but she is gone. I feel nothing except thirst. My mouth so dry my lips stick together. At night I curl up alone on the damp ground, waiting to die.

"Then the sun wake me. I am surprised to see another day. The Turks holler again, 'Yuru! Yuru! Gavurs!' Manoug is standing by the roadside and sees me. He has not seen Myreeg. He tries to feed me tiny pieces of bread, but I push it away because my throat iss too dry to swallow. He iss too weak to hold my hand and we are soon separated. I never see him again.

"I walk alone, weak and sick. By now my sandals are worn out and gone and the hot sands blister my feet, but they don't let us stop. The sand as far as I can see looks almost white to my blurring eyes. My feet scream out every time I step on that white sand. The stones in the sand are agony. I just think about water. I want water more than anything. I walk past dried-up dead bodies and I feel more sick. I have diarrhea for days, still wear same dress with no underwear. I throw up, there's diarrhea on me but I don't care. I want water.

"Maybe we walk another ten miles or more until we come to a place and stop. I don't know where. I'm so sick and weak my mind stop working and I lay on the ground. The next day I try to look for water but can't find any. I don't know what happened to my mother and I don't understand why she don't look for me. As we start to walk away from the town, a Turkish man walk up to the soldier and ask him to let him have me. The soldier take my hand and give me to the Turk, who walk me to his house. An Armenian lady, Rose, lived there with a daughter and two children. I find out later she save her life from Genocide by allowing her daughter to marry the Turkish man's brother-in-law. Rose take off my torn, filthy clothes, wash me and put on clean dress. I don't understand Turkish but Rose translate for me. She tell me I now live with the Halims and they give me new Turkish name, Jamulah.

"Couple weeks later Rose left with her two kids. Now there is no one to translate and the Halims and me don't understand each other, so I don't talk. I listen and try to learn Turkish words.

"For a month I can't eat much. Nothing stay down. I can't walk or even stand up, just lay on a cushion. When I start to eat a bit of food, I begin to feel better. But after that my eyes get sore and I can't open them. The Halims take me to a Turkish lady with new baby and she put her breast milk in my eyes, couple of times, but it doesn't help so they put pink powder in my eyes. It takes about a month to get better.

"All winter I do nothing. There is no one my age to play with or talk to so I just stay inside. Once I was asked to knead the bread dough by walking over it with bare feet. It was enough bread to last the entire winter. After six months I begin to learn Turkish words. One day Mrs. Halim tell me to wait outside our house while she go visit a neighbor. When Mr. Halim come home and find me standing there alone, he ask me, 'Where's your mother?' I don't like him calling her my mother, but I tell him she's at

the neighbor's. He tell me, 'Go tell her to come home.'
When she come they make me wait outside and I can hear
them arguing inside, he is angry with her for leaving me
alone. After he leave for work the next morning, she yell at
me, 'If I throw you in the toilet, nobody would miss you!'

"I so afraid I don't say a word. But life goes on. It is
fall of 1916 and I live there for one year already. One day
Mrs. Halim start to put a shelf near the ceiling for storing
bread. In Turkish she ask me for a hammer, but I don't
understand. She come down from the ladder with anger,
find a hammer and hit me over the head with it. I'm
bleeding but I can't cry or make a noise because she
threatens to hit me again. She sets fire to a rag and take
the ashes and put on my sore wound. She say, 'Don't you
dare tell your father about this or I will beat you again.' I
say nothing to him.

"She don't act mean to me for about six months, and
then one day she start to beat me again. This time she say,
'You steal my silver belt and give it away.' I don't know
enough Turkish to explain that I never saw it, don't know
anything about her silver belt. She start hitting me and
say, 'I beat you until you say, Yes, I take it.' So I move my
head yes, and she stop hitting me.

"When Mr. Halim come home that night he bring a
Turkish lady to visit. Mrs. Halim tell him I stole her silver
belt and gave it away. He ask me, 'Did you steal the belt?'
I nod my head yes because I'm afraid she beat me again.
For punishment, he held my hand to prick my finger with a
pin, but the visitor say something in Turkish to stop him.
The next morning Mr. Halim put some old clothes back on,
walked me to the town and asked each time we pass
someone if I gave that person the silver belt. I nod my head
yes every time. He left me at the police station where they
make me stand up in room all day without food or water.
In late afternoon, they send me home.

"When I get there Mrs. Halim tell me to wash myself
at the water pipe across the street. I go over and start to
wash, all I think about is how she hurt me, and I cry until
the tears wet my dress. Something inside me say run
away. I look around to see if they're watching me. No one
can see me so I start to walk away slowly, then faster until I
run, run for long time and then find an empty torn house

and hide myself in a dark hole under the porch. I am afraid of the dark but afraid of Halims more. Late at night it turns cold and dark. If anyone finds me there they might kill me or return me to the Halims, so I climb out and run to a house and knock on the door. A man opens it and stares at me. He looks at my filthy dress and slams the door and I run to the next house and knock. A Turkish woman opens the door and this time I tell her my name is Jamulah. She thinks I'm a Turkish beggar child and lets me in. She lives with another poor Turkish lady. They let me stay with them and sleep in their baby's room. They don't ask me any questions and I feel safe because of that."

Chapter 22

Victoria walked from the bench toward the overlook of Manhattan to watch the sun set. City lights beamed brightly for miles as tourists flocked to the windows in admiration of the New York skyline. Virginia sat alone on the bench noting the intimacy passing couples shared by smiling to the other or by holding hands; such simple gestures conveyed enormous feeling and yet to Virginia it was completely unnatural. She viewed such people with envy; their ease in giving themselves so freely was, even now, a foreign concept to her. "It all starts with outward affection," she thought to herself. "But how does one ever find the courage to be this trusting and uninhibited with another?"

She replayed the story over and over in her consciousness; Myreeg's constant threat of death and danger at every turn caused Virginia to feel lightheaded to a point where she had to grasp the bench rail for support. Slumped against the hard wood, she remained for ten minutes lost in private meditation, oblivious to all surroundings, including Myreeg. Her thoughts lingered on how little she knew of her own mother; the person who had given her life was quite literally a stranger, and this terrible story only served as a reminder. Why had Myreeg hidden this? Did she not trust her family? Virginia felt a wave of emotion surface; a mix of anger, sadness and despair toward all that might have been avoided if this openness and trust had come earlier, yet mingled with this was a renewed sense of hope that finally perhaps she and Myreeg might become closer. What lay ahead? How should she now act toward her mother knowing this past? How would Myreeg act toward her?

Myreeg returned from the window and sat quietly beside Virginia, leaving her to continue placing these new revelations into perspective. Five minutes later a nod from Virginia seemed sufficient signal to continue the story.

"It is spring of 1917. The two Turkish ladies I live with in Mezreh have an Armenian neighbor, Ahrax, with two daughters. Ahrax was not persecuted by the Turks because she was a converted Protestant, which means they have the backing and close communication with the American church. The Turks obviously didn't want to turn America against them, so most of the Protestant Armenians were spared. Anyway, the Turkish ladies send me often to borrow sugar from Ahrax, who always offer to feed because she know I do not have much food. I always shake my head no because I'm afraid that if I talk too much the Turks will find me and send me back to the Halims. One day she ask me if I'm Armenian and I shake my head no, but she repeats, 'You Armenian kid? Tell me and I will give you a doll.' When she say this, I shake my head yes. She assure me that when I come back next time she will give me a doll if I promise to come alone. I nod my head yes and leave in a run, very excited. All that day I am out in the field tending to the Turkish ladies' animals and I can only think about the doll and how I can't wait to get her. For three days I work in the field hoping for another chance to run an errand to Ahrax, but no one asks me, so on the fourth day I sneak away from the fields to see her. She tell me she doesn't have the doll and I am upset, so I cry. Ahrax put a finger to her lips as she begins to put baggy pants over my skirt and a shawl over my face so that only my eyes are seen. I am scared at what is happening, but make no sound. A man appears waiting in the doorway; he walk to me and take my arm to lead me out back door. I don't know where I'm going, but the man speak in Armenian to Ahrax and I feel a little better hearing my own language. We walk for half hour to American Near East Missionaries."

Virginia interrupted her. "I've read about those missionaries who attempted to convert the Muslims back in the early 1800s. It was declared illegal to convert any Turkish citizens, so the missionaries established a mission in Constantinople to serve other Christians in the area who were mostly Greek and Armenian. Later the missionaries founded four Armenian colleges in ancient Armenia, located in Aintab, Marash, Kharpet and Marsovan. The college in Kharpet was, if I remember, destroyed in World War I."

Victoria nodded. "I'm happy to be with missionaries in Kharpet because I am with Armenian orphans my age and we get to go to school together. The missionaries pay two Armenian sisters to take care of me until the orphanage, a decrepit and abandoned Armenian house, could open. That winter I am sick with white bumps all over my face. It is Dahrue, an ulcerative skin disease. The sisters take me to a doctor who rubs medicine on my face that burns real bad. I tremble and cry out from the pain, but next day the pain is gone, and so is the disease. Many sores remain which I pick at and eventually make bleed so much that the missionary doctor think my nose will fall off. One year goes by before it heals, but I still have nasty scar." She leaned over and touched it for Virginia's benefit.

"One day I learn that Rose, the Armenian lady who stayed with the Halims for awhile, live across the street from our orphanage. She see me playing on the porch and come over to tell the sisters that Mr. Halim want me back. The sisters ask me if I want to go back and I cry and holler, 'No! His wife beat me again.' Rose argued with them but they wouldn't let her have me, so she left real angry.

"The next morning the sisters shout at me from outside to go hide in the wine cellar. They say Mr. Halim is coming over to take me back with him. 'Don't be afraid,' they say. 'We will help you.'

"I run downstairs to hide and moments later hear footsteps and voices. I see Mr. Halim light a match, and he sees me hiding under a table. I come out, shaking, to kiss his hand and he take my arm and lead me upstairs. I am shivering as he say firmly, 'Jamulah, I take you home with me.' The two sisters stand behind him and say, 'Tourvanda, if you don't want to go, just say so,' and I say 'No.' Mr. Halim stand up, let go of me, say goodbye and disappear. I am shocked because I expect him to be angry and force me home, but he doesn't say anything. The two sisters give me a big hug and say, 'You are very brave, Tourvanda.'

"I'm so happy I don't have to go back to that mean wife, happy she can't beat me or accuse me of stealing anymore. I feel like I'm born again, thank God for the sisters."

"You were lucky," Virginia said. "So many doors opened for you—Mr. Halim rescued you from the March of Death, then the two Turkish ladies took you in on the night you ran away, after that Ahrax delivered you to the missionaries, and finally the two sisters gave you courage to say no to Mr. Halim."

Victoria nodded, then her face turned grim. "But my life continued to be a struggle to get enough to eat and stay warm. The two Armenian sisters go back after a year to their own village because food is so scarce. Sarah, an older Armenian orphan, moves in to live with me and we are nearly starving because the orphanage has so little money to feed us. One day I am playing on the sidewalk at my house and a Kurdish man walk up and say I am so skinny, would I like to go home with him for some food. I too young to know the danger, so I say yes and ride with him on the backside of a donkey to his house an hour away. We get there and when his wife see me she yell, 'I already got two Armenian orphans to feed and we don't have enough food for ourselves. Take her back!' She gives me a little water and lets me stay the night, but the next day the man walk me back to Kharpet. I am lucky he doesn't hurt me; I was so desperate for food I didn't care anymore who give it to me or the risks involved.

"Sometime in 1918, the Turkish landlord of our house come and ask Sarah for rent money. Sarah asks the head of the missionaries what to do, and he suggests we move into the newly established orphanage, which is another rundown Armenian house next door to ours and across the street from Yeprad College. This is the first orphanage in Kharpet, and me and Sarah are among first thirteen orphans to live there. After a few weeks the missionaries find more and more Armenian children in Turkish home, brought in under circumstances similar to mine. Missionaries remove them from the Turkish homes to bring into our orphanage. Before long there are twenty-five and the missionaries have even less money to feed all of us. We manage a small piece of bread and soup made from boiled cabbage twice a day.

"On Sundays a few of the orphans went to the Armenian church. Since no one had their own shoes to wear into the church, we share several secondhand pairs from the orphanage, passing them along to each kid so that everyone can go at a different time. We are always still hungry, but the housemother tell us that prayer will help us to forget our hunger, so at night we cry and pray, turn over and over on the floor until we fall asleep."

Virginia said, "Now I understand why you always made us eat everything on our dinner plates. When I was little I always thought that your complaints of starving were just to get us to eat; I didn't believe you really had starved. I can't imagine what you went through; I remember when I was dieting, I tried fasting one day and it was agony—all I could think of and smell was food."

Victoria nodded. "It really happened, Vehrsheen and it was difficult. You never forget what it's like to starve. That's why I always thankful for food on our table and why I never let it go to waste. Finding food was always our first concern and as the missionaries bring more and more orphans, the food shortage is more critical. Due to all the new orphans coming, five more orphanages open near us. Still, there is little food and the incoming orphans arrive with bugs and lice due to poor care or neglect in Turkish homes and soon it gets passed to all of us because there is no bathing water and we only get to go to Turkish baths once a month. We get our drinking water from a neighbor's rusted water pipe across the street. My head is infested with lice and I can't sleep at night.

"I still always think about how much I want my doll so one day I make one from an old twig shaped like a wishbone and a few dishrags I find in the house. I pretend my doll is Norah; I talk and play with her, just like Norah and I did in our village. Whenever I go outside I hide Norah behind some steps in the house so that no one will take her away from me like the Turks took away the real Norah.

"In the summertime it is hot so we take our mats out onto the flat roof and sleep under the stars. Sometimes it rains so we race to pick up our blankets and run into the house. That was fun.

"In the winter we have no wood to burn, so we use yellow Goldenrod flowers picked in the fall instead. The housemother ties the flowers onto the side of the house to dry out in the sun, and then in wintertime we burn them in the stove. We have no sweaters or coats, so we all stay in one room bunched together, straining to feel what little heat comes from the stove.

"On New Year's Day, 1918, the missionaries put up a little Christmas tree with a few Christmas balls on it. They had no money for gifts but we get nuts and raisins and sing Armenian songs. That was the first Christmas I celebrate away from my family. Because I was with Muslims the year before, we didn't celebrate and I was too scared to even think about it. The orphanage tries to make Christmas fun but it only make us miss our families and we are sad."

Chapter 23

The sun had set over Ellis Island and the New York nightlife was getting into full gear. Victoria and Virginia both left the Statue of Liberty drained from the storytelling and eager to escape it for awhile. They visited an outdoor café in Rockefeller Center for dinner, where neither ate much but instead eyed the street merchants going about selling their wares to the endless flow of people stopping to survey the products. Virginia focused on the faces in the nameless crowds thinking of how impossible it was to determine a person's past solely from outward appearances or everyday contact. She'd spent forty-three years with Myreeg and all throughout there was never even a thought of such a grim, intense past. It was impossible to guess at such a life based upon Myreeg's prior outward appearances and actions, and yet at the same time, her actions seemed in keeping with this past. It was easy to see why she'd been so insistent on finishing meals, of her lack of affection and trust. The threat of betrayal was all too often a possibility and survival demanded acting solely on her instincts, and avoiding intimacy with others because their death was as big a threat as hers, and the situation was such that she could not concern herself with the fate of others. Further, the risk of losing someone close was very real and she'd obviously been shaken from the loss of her entire family. It made sense she wouldn't allow herself to become close to anyone, their loss would be too much for her to bear. Myreeg had been raised alone in an unforgiving world where her violent childhood served to ultimately shape her adult life. To Virginia, she did not seem to fully trust or confide in her husband or children, perhaps from fear of losing them as she did her own family. Every detail of her past in Armenia was steeped in worry; life or death was at every corner and even the smallest of actions had to be taken seriously and with utmost caution. Life in America was approached much the same way: harmless everyday experiences like housecleaning were taken with complete solemnity and constant worry. A disorderly house to Victoria meant chaos.

Keeping Virginia at a distance by criticizing was in fact a defense for not letting her get close, and not a dislike, as Virginia often thought. As a child and later adult she took an antagonistic approach as a defense for this feeling of unwantedness, finding a certain pride from disobeying Myreeg whenever possible. She realized within herself that Myreeg would never have told this story if she really disliked her. It was impossible to resist speculation of how things might have been different if this story had become family knowledge. Would Virginia have taken an antagonistic attitude as a child? Might she have shown more respect and not be so put off by the criticisms? Hearing this story placed her own childhood in perspective as to why she grew up having difficulty becoming close with school friends, and later, intimate with boyfriends. She shared many of her mother's traits of constant worry and distrust, her reservations and shyness. After all attempts to not be like Myreeg, in the end she'd taken on the very same characteristics she sought to avoid. Emotions of anger, despair and sadness were the only familiar ones which Myreeg could genuinely show, and thus they were the only emotions Virginia came to know in her everyday living environment. She approached many situations as did her mother: with constant worry and a lack of self-confidence. Her prospective move to California was nixed because of her worry over Myreeg's disapproval; her canceled engagement to Sean was due to her worry over her parents' disapproval. Myreeg was almost a complete stranger to her and yet was the person she felt closest to. There was an inseparable bond between them—in the end Virginia always returned to Myreeg. It was Myreeg's word that prompted a decision, Myreeg's word was the one she obeyed above all others. In the end her own identity had been compromised by obeying and clinging to Myreeg. The two women were unmistakably united by this story but the past held many wounds between them which could never be changed or forgotten in the short time Myreeg had left to her. What existed now was a conflict: how should they both carry on knowing and acknowledging Myreeg's past? Would Myreeg trust her more, show more affection and openness? Would Virginia not be as antagonistic? Every action henceforth took on a new importance. Building a solid, trusting relationship was the goal, yet both were firmly set in their ways which made change difficult.

As coffee was served Victoria resumed her story.

"My group of orphans moved to Kesierig in the spring of 1919; we walk the half hour distance from Kharpet. The Turks had overtaken many of the abandoned Armenian houses throughout the Genocide, which made it hard for the missionaries to establish an orphanage. One such abandoned dwelling appeared capable of housing thirty children, so the head missionary set out to convince the Turk living there to leave through a generous bribe. There was no way legally under Turkish law to get him to move out and if the case somehow got to court a Christian had no hope of winning against a Muslim. The bribe eventually got him to move.

"In Kesierig we go to the fields and pick wild vegetables and fruit. There is a river where we jump in and swim often; we always so excited to be in cool water that we forget to take our clothes off first. We laugh and splash each other—it was the most fun I had for a very long time. In August of that summer I had a bad scare. One afternoon our housemother, Mrs. Tashjian, ask me to bring tomatoes to her from the garden that our orphanage boys had made. I go to the field and ask boys to pick some tomatoes for Mrs. Tashjian while I wait in a tiny wood and clay shack, because it is too hot to stay outside. While I wait some orphanage boys throw heavy blocks of wood and rocks onto the roof which make it cave in. I hear them run away laughing. I am trapped underneath clay boards and can't get my breath, not even enough to yell once. I'm afraid I will die, but the boys in the garden see the roof cave in and run to yank the boards off. They find me and pull my legs to drag me outside, where I catch my breath and thank them for saving me. Those boys were my friends. I didn't have any physical injury, but I was scared for long time after. I never told on those boys and they never bother me again.

"About a month later I had another problem. I am always cold and shake and shiver constantly. After a little while, I feel hot and my body burn. My stomach swell like a pregnant lady even though I am skinny so I go to Dr. Jacobson, a missionary, who make me swallow a gray pill shaped like an egg. In a few days I throw up a five-inch tapeworm, but after that my stomach go down and I feel much better.

"In the fall of 1919, the missionaries move us back to Mezreh and open school there. We move into another abandoned Armenian house, where downstairs there is a kitchen and living room. Every morning we eat bean soup in a clay bowl and half a slice of bread for lunch, and more soup for dinner. There are five rooms upstairs where at night we put our flat cushions on the floor and cover up in quilts. One tall orphan girl from a village near Mezreh sing us sad Armenian songs and we all cry. In the middle of the night Turks from the village come knock on our door to threaten us. The housemother is always afraid they will kill us, since they already kill one of our boys.

"We are still hungry all the time and we cry in the night until our eyes hurt before wiping our tears away come daytime to play outside in hopes of forgetting our hunger. The housemother send all the orphans into the orchards to collect tree branches to burn for winter. There is one small wood-burning stove for six rooms, so at night fifteen of us gather around and fight to be near the heat. In the afternoon we fold our bed clothes and store them on shelves on the wall so we can hold school in that room. In school we don't have paper or pencil, we just go to the board and write our arithmetic answers in front of the class. Our teacher is Veronica Azarian and my best friend is Seeronoosh Tookoian. I am at school three years. In June of 1921 I receive my elementary education diploma. I am thirteen. I am excited to graduate because I remember that the class from last year wear beautiful flower garlands because the missionaries run out of money and can't afford to have nice ceremony, so they just pass out diplomas. I went out anyway and found my own flowers to wear which weren't as pretty as the garland but they still smell nice. It

was the best day of my life. My diploma is neatly tied with
red string, passing from Miss Veronica's hand into mine.
She smiles at me and whispers, 'Tourvanda, you look like a
princess.' I still have that diploma, locked away in that
dusty old suitcase you pestered me about long ago."

Virginia looked up at her. "What do you keep in that
suitcase anyway, Myreeg? I've always wondered since you
never use it for vacations or travel."

"No secrets. Just my Armenian Bible and diploma
from the orphanage, my passport, an empty box of King
George chocolates, some Egyptian coins, a few letters from
Cousin Harry, some postcards, a dresser cover I embroidered at Ellis Island along with some extra silk threads, a
photo of my girlfriends in the orphanage as well as one of
Cousin Dick and Harry together.

"I go to high school, which is another room in the
orphanage, in the fall of 1921. The Turks insist that
Turkish be taught, so we had three lessons before they
order school closed for no obvious reason. Anyway, the
missionaries grew disgusted because Turks continually
harass us by closing the schools, so eventually in 1922
over 22,000 Armenian orphans are moved out of the remote
interior of Turkey. We are lucky because there are many
other Armenian children who grew up to be Turks, who
never know their real identity.

"Twice a month the missionaries move thousands of
orphans out of Western Armenia by hay wagons to Syria
and Greece; my group consists of forty wagons with nine
girls in each; the boys go in separate wagons. We travel
over four hundred miles through many cities in about six
weeks on our way to Greece. About ten thousand
altogether were sent there. Every morning during the trip
the missionaries give us small piece of toast and cheese.
The Turkish government inspect the wagons regularly to
make sure outsiders do not mix with us. We wait in each
town until missionaries prepare room in next town. They
give out white cotton pointed hats to wear to protect us
from the hot sun. Each time we are about to enter a new
town, we spend the first night on the outskirts sleeping on
the ground while our head missionary goes to make sure
town is safe for us.

"We begin in Mezreh and go to Goldjik, from there to Arhans Maden. We go to the beautiful ancient Armenian city of Dikranagerd, built years before Christ by our King Tigran. It is a walled city on the Tigris River which was inhabited by Armenians. The Turks later change the name to Diyabekir. From Diyabekir we went on to Severag. We stop at Ourfa and the missionaries bring us grapes and eggplant stew—I remember it is first time I have this stew, and I like it very much because it is hot and spicy. I dream of that stew on nights when I am hungry; I can smell and taste it for days.

"When we travel in the wagons, we are with different children each time. At night I am lonely so I go looking for my friends and always find them, so we can all lay together and say our prayers before falling asleep. I wake up in the morning feeling much better and return to my assigned wagon. We travel south toward the Euphrates River where we leave the hay wagons behind for a large truck which take us to Aleppo, Syria. We are packed in close together and it is very hot inside. When we leave Turkey, the truck driver turns to us and smiles, 'You're free now! No Turks here. Don't be afraid. Sing, be happy!'

"We are all happy to get out of Turkey, but there are too many of us packed into one truck so we wait until we get out before celebrating.

"We arrive in Aleppo at nighttime. All the city lights are on, which is nice because none of us see electric lights before. We sleep in a bathhouse for a week and then ride a train up the Mediterranean to Antillias, a port in Beirut, in mid July. The water is as blue as the sky, there are no clouds for the sun to hide behind and I shade my eyes to look across the sea, so wide that I can't see other side. In Antillias we stay in buildings facing out to the Mediterranean and are given tea and rolls for breakfast. We play in a cold stream nearby with out clothes on and then run through the building to the other side to get to the warm sea. We always splash each other because the warm water is so soothing and it is easy to forget hunger and loneliness. We stay for two and a half months. It is heaven.

"In the middle of October, 1922, fifteen hundred of us are put aboard an old coal freighter going to Istanbul, where we will get a ship to Greece sometime before Christmas. At first I'm afraid to go back to Turkey but someone say Istanbul has lots of powerful, sympathetic Westerners who Turks didn't want to make angry, so we are pretty safe. There are no beds on the freighter so we sleep on decks black from coal shipments. A storm hit that night, throwing us from side to side on the deck and the waves spill over our screams and prayers. I am afraid we are going to die.

"The next evening we arrive in Istanbul safely and the American missionaries give us baths, clean clothes and haircuts. They feed and put us to bed and in the morning give us breakfast. Since we will be here for couple months, the missionaries make school to teach us the English alphabet and words. Before Christmas we get our ship to the Greek Island of Aidhipsou where we stay in a mineral spa complete with hot springs for bathing. Tangerine trees with small white flowers grow all over the beautiful island. One drachma gets you a dozen tangerines. Whenever an orphan has money to buy them, we share with everyone. It tastes sweet, juicy, and delicious.

"Couple of weeks later the missionaries bring orphans from Sepastia, Western Armenia. One girl from that group want to know if there's any orphans from Divirig and they tell her I am from there. I am so excited to find out who else might be from there and I go with a girlfriend to see. I am surprised to find my childhood friend Kaleesta Kochyan from my old village of Palanga.

"'Oh, Kaleesta! Thank God! I'm so happy to see you!' We hug each other, cry and spend a long time talking about our families and what we have been through. She is sixteen and I am fourteen.

"Kaleesta say, 'My mother told me your cousin Dick returned to Istanbul from America in 1920 looking for his wife and son and the rest of his family, but found out they were all dead. While he was still in Istanbul he married an Armenian lady.'

"I tell Kaleesta I didn't get to Istanbul until 1922, but this was happy news for me because I didn't know I had any living relatives.

"While Kaleesta tell me this good news, Violet Manedian, another orphan, is listening. She say her uncle in Chicago can help me find Cousin Dick. She say I should write a letter so he can print it in the Armenian newspapers across America.

"I tell her that is good idea and thank her. I sit and write the letter at once, sending it off with my picture. It turns out, by luck, that Violet's uncle and my cousin Harry had worked together in Ohio in 1913 after first arriving in America. Because he knew Cousin Harry personally, Violet's Uncle Aram sent my letter and picture directly to Harry in New York. It is May, 1923, and I am fifteen. One day while I am washing my hair with Seeronoosh, many girls run to me excited. They shout, 'Congratulation, Tourvanda! Congratulations!' I do not know why they say this to me but I begin to understand when one girl hand me letter from Cousin Harry. I open the envelope and read the letter out loud. Cousin Harry ask me to write back to identify myself by naming the people in my family and relatives. I write to him that day giving my parents' names, brother and sister. I shut my eyes tight and say a prayer before dropping the envelope into the mail, hoping that Cousin Harry will send an answer back very quick. I think maybe this be the first step to America.

"Several months later, I get back a letter.

July 22, 1923

Dear Cousin Turan Ahigian

I received your letter dated 4th of the month. When we received word of your survival we decided to find means to help you. Don't ever think that your brothers are indifferent toward you. Prior to this letter we sent you another letter and enclosed were ten dollars and a photograph of us. We are waiting for a response to that letter.

Now this letter, as soon as you receive it and read it carefully, you will see that it will be helpful to you. We have prepared your affidavit and purchased your boat ticket. With this letter you will receive the whole package in an envelope. After receiving the papers, go present them immediately to the agent. The agent's address is on the envelope. There you must get only a passport and the agent will tell you how to acquire it. If the agent doesn't tell you, you can find out from the Americans by telling them that your uncles from America have sent an invitation to come to America. Find out from him as to where you can secure your passport. When they ask you where you'll be staying in America, you tell them you'll be residing at Minas Giragosian's address. Show the card you will receive. This is my address. If they ask you who this person is tell them he's your uncle. Don't give them our name. Don't say you are going to your brother's address. Show that card. If they ask you how many years he has been living in America, tell them twenty years. Tell them that when you were young, your mother would tell you that your uncle was in America. When speaking be careful you don't say anything wrong. If they ask you additional questions tell them you were young and thus don't know. Tell them only that you had given your name to a newspaper and that your uncle had seen your name and invited you to America. Send us a telegram immediately.

Dikran and Haroutioun Ahigian

P.S. Take good care of your papers, your affidavit, your boat ticket, and the card. Don't tell even your friends about this letter. Only you read it. If your friends ask, tell them your uncle has called for

you and that you are going to America.
The boat ticket is good for one year;
don't lose it. As soon as you receive this
letter, find out from the agent the name
of the boat company and the American
Consul about your trip. Tell us immediately what they say. Don't worry. As
long as we're alive, whatever problems
you may have, let us know. Don't be
bashful. With this letter you'll receive a
twenty dollar check. If that money is not
enough for your passport...

"I can't believe it is happening. I am going to
America.

"Miss Cushman, who was in charge of the orphans
and knew all the immigration regulations, say when she
hear of my leaving, 'You can't go, Tourvanda. The quotas to
America are closed for this year.'

"'What do you mean?' I cry.

"'The legitimate government agents issue the quota
numbers and they have already been filled for 1923. I'm so
sorry, Tourvanda, but they won't allow you into the
country. They'll just send you back here. Maybe you can
go next year.'

"With that I bury my hopes for America and send the
boat ticket back to Cousin Harry, explaining that the
quotas are closed for now and that I will be all right at the
orphanage."

Chapter 24

"In the spring of 1923 I am sad because we leave Aidhipsou. It is prime tourist season and many visitors enjoy coming to the mineral spas, so we must go to make room for paying visitors. We move to Corintos, (Corinth) Greece which take us a day of travel by boat. When we arrive the missionaries give us clothes and blankets with a number stamped on each. My number is 909. There is no shelter for us so we sleep under the stars at night, using old cushions as substitute for beds. It is very hot in Corintos and none of us have shoes so we walk barefoot over the hot sands. The water is not safe to drink, but we have no other water source so we drink anyway, and many of the orphans get sick with diarrhea, three even die. The missionaries set up one big tent for all of the sick orphans during that summer. I am made a nurse since I am not sick, and I deliver food and medicine to many orphans.

"In the fall they move us to Greek army barracks where we sleep and have school. During my final exams in high school I hear guns firing near our building from the ongoing Civil War in Greece. I am sick and unable to study for a week, and the principal ask me why I don't study my lessons. I'm too shy to tell him I don't feel good, so I study even though my head aches because I'm afraid to be scolded.

"We didn't have a tree for Christmas but the missionaries give us raisins and nuts. We sing Armenian Protestant Christmas songs and the missionaries give us each an Armenian Bible for a Christmas present. It is the Bible I keep in my suitcase. We read stories from it in class to learn about our religion; each of us retell a story from it to the class.

"We stay in Corintos for a year and a half. The missionaries give us each a small cloth bag to keep our comb and other small items from getting lost. There is not enough money to take care all of us, so they cut down on school, making it half day every day. In the winter of 1925 they divide us up again, sending us all over the world except Turkey. I go with thirteen orphan girls to Alexandria, Egypt, separated from all my friends. Up to now I realize my life is not so bad because I am with friends. But when I move to Egypt, I am lonely. We ride over by boat, the trip last one day. When we get there the missionaries take us to St. Paul and Peter's Armenian Church with a stone wall around it and two big iron doors. The church director needs money to help other orphans so we are hired by families to work as maids or servants in exchange for a few gold coins and a place to live.

"They place me with an Italian family as a maid, which makes me ashamed. I don't understand Italian and am unable to speak for three months until I can learn some of the language. They make me eat my meals alone in the kitchen which make me even more lonely. Once a week they make me deliver macaroni to the Arabic bakery to be cooked in ovens, which is where I met a Syrian lady one day. She ask in Italian, 'Do you go to school?'

"I say, 'No, I am orphan girl working for the Italian family across the street.'

"'Would you like to live with my family instead, and take care of my son Lulu?'

"I say yes when she tell me I don't have to do house-work. I go back to the Italian family's house and luckily only the blind grandmother is home, so I threw my clothes out the window and slip out the front door.

"I live with the Syrian family for year and a half, a happy time. They are kind to me but still I eat alone and I hate that. But the Syrian lady give me needlework lessons and I make lace trim for the top and hem of my slip, which I keep in my suitcase. During the day when I take care of three year old Lulu, I secretly teach him Armenian words.

"At Christmas time the Syrian family doesn't put up a Christmas tree but they bake lots of fancy cookies and other fine foods. They give me a British guinea, which is

equal to one dollar, and I buy myself a Christmas present—
the suitcase.

"By 1927 I am tired of living with strangers and
restless to go to America to be with my cousins Dick and
Harry. It has been three years since Cousin Harry has sent
me the boat ticket, but I write him again to ask to be
brought over as a visitor, hoping that there is a way for me
to stay once I get there. While I wait for Cousin Harry's
response I move back to the church sanctuary owned by
Armenians, to live with a few other orphans and prepare
my papers for America.

"I hear from Cousin Harry a few weeks later and he
say my visit is a good idea. He send me some visitor papers
and three hundred dollars with instructions to find a
passport and birth certificate. This is a problem for me
since I have no citizenship, but I hear from friends that
there is a man named Mr. Tersian who gives false Egyptian-
born certificates to orphans for three hundred dollars. I
find him and give my money without getting a receipt and
wait months to hear that papers are ready. When I don't
hear anything I tell some girlfriends, who say he take
money from many orphans and don't do anything. 'Quick,'
they say, 'Go get your money back.'

"I tell my dentist, Dr. Simonian, my problem and
that I will report Mr. Tersian to the Archbishop, but the
dentist say he will get money back for me. Dr. Simonian
find Mr. Tersian and threaten him. Three months later I
get my money back.

"Meanwhile, I am busy preparing my passport
papers whenever I have a free moment. Soon, all I need is
a signature on my visa from the American Consul to make
it valid. They say I don't need birth certificate for passport,
only the signature. The Consul refuse to sign and I don't
understand why, so I run to the church director, Mr.
Lexian, who shake his head and says he can do nothing.

"In tears I plead with him. 'My girlfriend left for
America two weeks ago on a visitor's visa. Why do they
sign hers and not mine?'

"He say, 'Go home and I will look into it for you.'
Two weeks later Mr. Lexian say I need proof of family to
sponsor me and that the family must have stable jobs so
that I will not become a burden on the government should I

become sick while visiting or if something should happen to me there.   Mr. Lexian and other missionaries talk with Consulate of my case and say I have no living relatives here but that I have two cousins in New York with steady jobs who would sponsor me. After they meet, Mr. Lexian tell me the Consul will sign. I am so happy after that; I run to the Consul that day and when the signature is on my visa I thank God for helping me.

"But there is more to be done; through Mr. Lexian I buy a third class ticket overseas for one hundred and fifty dollars. He tell me to keep fifty dollars cash for when I arrive in New York and put the remainder of my money toward a new dress and a pair of good shoes. I have a cheap dress made, and buy shoes; also buy two gold pens which I give to the Archbishop, Sooren Mampreian, and Mr. Lexian in thanks for them watching over me and helping.

"On the day I am to leave, I rent a horse and buggy to drive to the wharf where I will take a British ship called the *White Star* on its maiden voyage. I give my last fifteen dollars Egyptian currency to the orphanage for my friends to have a nice dinner from me. A couple of my girlfriends ride to the port to wish me luck in finding a way to stay in America permanently. They give me a box of King George chocolates and say, 'Find us good husbands, Tourvanda, so we can come to America too.' I am so excited to leave that I barely say goodbye before beginning to climb a narrow rope ladder onto the ship. When I get on board I wave one last time to my friends, promising to find them all rich Armenian husbands in America.

"My room is on the lowest deck. My cabinmate is a girl my age from Italy named Rachel, who is traveling from Egypt back to her homeland. In the morning Rachel and I walk the lower deck to the bow of the ship and watch sharks race alongside us. We walk about the deck and see hundreds of immigrants all going to America. Everyone looks the same I think, full of hope and fear of living in America.

"We reach Naples, Italy, on the third day and Rachel says goodbye, leaving the cabin to me. I don't like being alone again because I begin to worry about being sent back. At least when I have roommate I can talk so I won't worry.

"In the morning I walk upstairs to the deck and see the deep blue sky. No birds. No sound. No trees or land. The water is calm, and I feel a little relaxed, like maybe someone will help me stay in America. The trip lasts nineteen days. I still don't eat well, but I meet a Greek lady and husband who make me eat breakfast with them. After that, trip not so terrible because it's not so lonely. We dock in New York Harbor on March 4, 1928 at four a.m. It was very dark and foggy over the ocean so I don't see the Statue from my cabin window. I think suddenly of my mother, brother and sister and I begin to cry. It is very happy moment for me yet at the same time I am sad that my family is not with me to experience this great joy. I think of them all and wonder where they are and wish that my family could be with me to experience this exciting moment. I feel both happy and sad at the same time.

"Suddenly the ship lurches into port. I take off my old dress, my Armenian orphan dress, and put on the new one I bought the day I leave Egypt. I crumple the old one up into ball, open the cabin window and throw it into the ocean. I walk up the deck and find my way to the front, anxious to find my cousins and new life in America."

Chapter 25

It was dusk when Victoria and Virginia finally pulled in the driveway of their home, the safe, modest, red brick house that Myreeg was so proud of. It was a long distance from her homeland; wall-to-wall carpeting replaced dirt floors. Away from the orphanage, the deserts, the uncertainty. Virginia was also glad to be home, for the story of her mother's past had been upsetting. It had left her shaken, but now that they were home she could begin to contemplate the meaning of all of this.

Michael ran out to greet them. "How was the trip?" he asked eagerly. They went into the house, taking turns relating the visit to New York and Ellis Island.

During the next few days Virginia could not take her thoughts away from her mother's story of the suffering, the loneliness, and the pain. As difficult as Virginia's life had been growing up in Michigan, her mother's had been even more so. She could not believe her mother was capable of enduring so much pain, constant danger, and the threat of violence. Yet Myreeg had persevered and had succeeded. In a way her story was an inspiration; she had defied insurmountable odds and risen above a darkness so profound that only the strong could hope to survive. And she did survive. But to survive she had to suppress her feelings. To allow feelings of family lost, of dreams shattered, would have destroyed her altogether. So she learned to feel nothing, and that is how she survived. It was also why Myreeg could not show affection, why she could not get close to people and have friends. It was why she offered criticisms and complaints to Vehrsheen; this had managed to keep them both distant and yet never apart.

Yet as bravely as Myreeg fought to survive, as in any battle, there were injuries, and Virginia could not help but wonder how the scars of her mother's battles had been passed down to her. It became clear that Myreeg's discouragement for having Virginia leave home was out of her own insecurity of being alone again and without family.

Three weeks after they had arrived home, a letter came from Val, Virginia's old college roommate, saying she was coming to Michigan from Chicago and hoped that they could have lunch together. Virginia was so excited, she rummaged through the boxes in the basement to find her college yearbook to look up Valerie's picture. "What fun it will be to reminisce!" she told Myreeg.

Virginia dressed herself in the old maize and blue sweater before meeting Valerie at an old Ann Arbor hangout, The Sugarbowl. They both recognized the other and each said they hadn't changed in the twenty years since college. Virginia noticed that Val had a beautiful navy suit with gold buttons and a luscious brown fur coat casually thrown over her shoulders. A big diamond ring graced her third finger, left hand.

Val started laughing. "You're still a funny one, Virginia," referring to her yellow pleated skirt and college sweater with a big U of M badge sewn on the front. She flushed at the reference to her clothes but covered by jumping up and pretending to be a cheerleader. "Hail to the Victors valiant, Hail to the conquering heroes..." They both giggled and Virginia sat down.

"Val, look what I brought." She opened a yearbook to a page with the two of them pictured. "Remember this shot?" It was a picture of them doing their musical act, "Side by Side." Both girls laughed at the photo and began talking of old times. Finally, after a pause, Val asked, "What have you been doing all these years? Not married, I see," referring to her finger. "Too many men to choose from, I bet."

"No," Virginia replied. "I never got that kissing thing down pat." They both laughed.

The waiter came for their orders and they both had a salad. "Oh, let's have some wine, too, and toast to the good old days, Val. And to all the boys who could have loved us then. Those lucky dogs!" They both giggled. "Yes, waiter, please bring us a carafe of white wine."

A moment passed. "Virginia, how are your parents? Do they still come over and visit you often, like in school?"

Virginia winced. "Well, Val, my mother isn't too well. I've been living at home just to make sure everything is all right." Virginia hesitated and neglected to say that after college she'd lived at home for most of the time. "Anyway, it's worked out well because it lets me save money for travel, you know, to interesting places."

"Well," Val said, "here's our wine, Virginia. Let's toast to old times."

"No, how about to old times and to new times as well? That would be good, don't you think?" Val laughed and touched her glass to Virginia's. They drank the wine and Val filled their glasses again. The salads arrived.

"So, Val, tell me what your life is like in Chicago."

"Oh, life has been pretty good to me, Virginia, not perfect, but then whose is! I brought you a surprise." She started rummaging through her sleek handbag. "Ah, here they are." She handed an envelope to Virginia. "Look inside."

Virginia opened the envelope to find pictures of four beautiful blond, blue-eyed children, all immaculately dressed and smiling.

"Yes, Virginia, they're mine. After school I worked in Chicago and married Terry, the tall guy." She laughed. "The girl next to him is my daughter, Jennifer. She looks a lot like I did when I was in college, doesn't she? Well, anyway, he swept me off my feet. We have so much in common. We both love to go boating on Lake Michigan— the boat in this picture here is ours that we take every summer to the lake. We've many friends in Chicago whom we see often. We still manage to dance a lot. I could never give up dancing. The next photo is of the house on Lake Michigan."

Virginia was struck by the likeness of the boat to Sean's boat.

"Now these, Virginia, are my two darling grand-children. Their father is Bill, my oldest son who is on his way to becoming a doctor. He loves children. And this is my middle son, the accountant, David. My youngest son Michael is a wizard with computers."

"What a great family," Virginia exclaimed, looking away from the photos and sighing. She was beginning to feel uncomfortable and knew it wasn't from the wine. She took a few bites of a hard boiled egg. She could hardly swallow.

"Yes," Val said. "It was hard in the early years when Terry was starting his business, and I was pregnant every year and a half. But we toughed it out and like anything you work hard at, it eventually turns out. They're all great kids, and Terry and I get along better now than ever before."

Virginia felt her stomach tense at reference to a happy marriage. They talked some more, but Virginia's discomfort was getting worse. Suddenly Val quickly stood. "My God! I was supposed to meet Terry a half hour ago. I have to run, Virginia. It's been so great to see you again. Now, no argument—I'll pay."

"Then I'll leave the tip," Virginia offered. They got up to exit. Val wrapped her fur coat around her shoulders and walked quickly to the door.   Virginia followed slowly behind, still not feeling well.

At their cars, the girls hugged and promised not to let so much time pass by, and Virginia promised to visit whenever she got to Chicago. They parted company.

Virginia drove back home very slowly, her stomach in knots, her eyes unable to focus straight ahead at the highway. Everything was blurred. Thoughts of her mother starving on the desert...thoughts of Val's luxurious life on Lake Michigan...thoughts of Sean's boat and Aram's painful disappointment swirled in her head. She could hardly breathe—a single tear trickled down her cheek. She drove up to the safe familiar red-brick colonial house with the plush wall-to-wall carpeting and the attached two car garage, realizing at that very moment there had been two orphans in the sands.

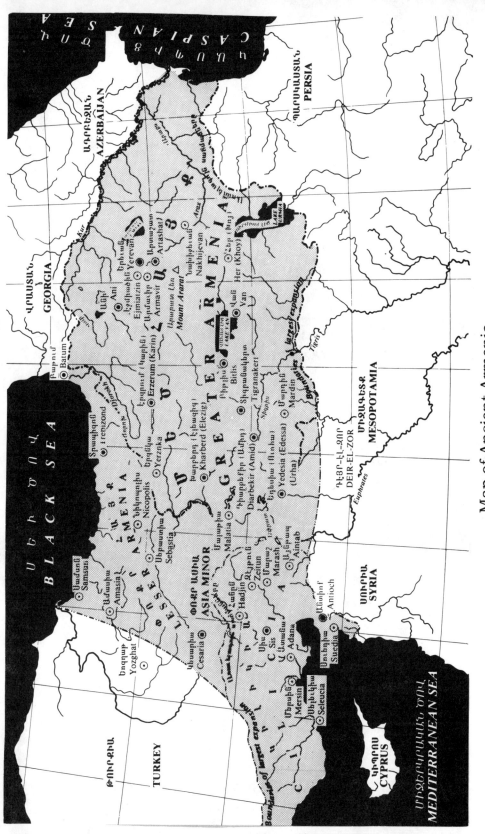

Map of Ancient Armenia

Tourvanda's elementary diploma from the
orphanage in Mezreh, June 14, 1921.

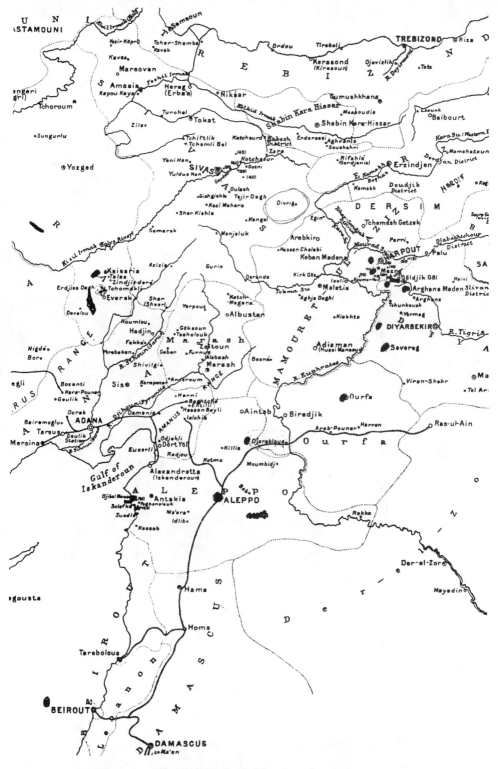

Places missionaries detained orphans
during their exodus from Turkey in 1922.

Λουτρὰ Αἰδηψοῦ

Dormitories for orphans in Aidhipsou, Greece, 1923.

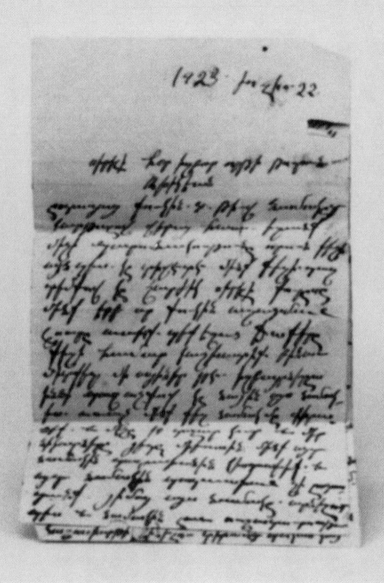

Cousin Harry's letter to Tourvanda
explaining immigration procedures.

Tourvanda Ahigian
Photo Tourvanda sent to her
cousins in America, 1923.

Cousins Harry and Dick Ahigian
Photo sent to Tourvanda for recognition
when she was in the orphanage, 1923.

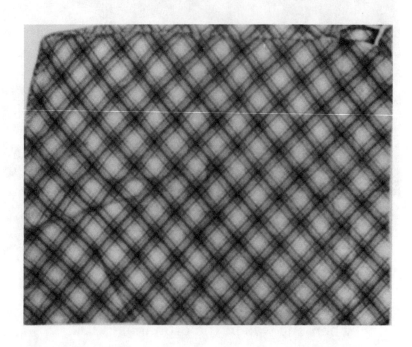

Armenian Bible and cloth tote bag
given to orphans in Corinth, Greece, 1924.

Tourvanda's needlework
Alexandria, Egypt, 1925.

Tourvanda's suitcase.

Archbishop Sooren Mampreian

Tourvanda's Passport.

KING GEORGE
CHOCOLATES
CADBURY BOURNVILLE ENG.   1 lb. Net.

WHITE STAR LINE

TRIPLE-SCREW S.S. "LAURENTIC."
19,000 TONS.

Tourvanda embroidered dresser cover at Ellis Island, 1928.

Michael and Victoria Haroutunian

Ahigian Family
From left to right: Ester, Mergiditch, Donnig, Harry,
Cousin Harry, Helen, Norah, Cousin Dick's first wife.

Seeronoosh Tookoian and Victoria Haroutunian
December, 1995.